Chemistry and Other Stories

ALSO BY RON RASH

NOVELS

One Foot in Eden

Saints at the River

The World Made Straight

SHORT FICTION

The Night the New Jesus Fell to Earth

Casualties

POETRY

Eureka Mill

Among the Believers

Raising the Dead

Chemistry and Other Stories

RON RASH

PICADOR

New York

www.picadorusa.com

Book design by Mary A. Wirth

Picador® is a U.S. registered trademark and is used by Henry Holt and Company
under license from Pan Books Limited.

For information on Picador Reading Group Guides, as well as ordering, please contact Picador.
Phone: 646-307-5629 Fax: 212-253-9627 E-mail: readinggroupguides@picadorusa.com

The following stories from this collection have been previously published elsewhere:
"Their Ancient, Glittering Eyes" and "Speckled Trout" in *The Kenyon Review;* "Last Rite" in *The
Greensboro Review;* "Overtime" in *The News & Observer* (Charleston); "Dangerous Love" in *South
Carolina Review;* "Cold Harbor" in *Shenandoah;* "Deep Gap" in *The Chattahoochee Review.*

ISBN-13: 978-0-312-42508-1
ISBN-10: 0-312-42508-2

First Edition: May 2007

10 9 8 7 6 5 4 3 2 1

For my daughter,

CAROLINE

Contents

Chemistry and Other Stories

Their Ancient, Glittering Eyes

Because they were boys, no one believed them, including the old men who gathered each morning at the Riverside Gas and Grocery. These retirees huddled by the potbellied stove in rain and cold, on clear days sunning out front like reptiles. The store's middle-aged owner, Cedric Henson, endured the trio's presence with a resigned equanimity. When he'd bought the store five years earlier, Cedric assumed they were part of the purchase price, in that way no different from the leaky roof and the submerged basement whenever the Tuckaseegee overspilled its banks.

The two boys, who were brothers, had come clattering across the bridge, red-faced and already holding their arms apart as if carrying huge, invisible packages. They stood gasping a few moments, waiting for enough breath to tell what they'd seen.

"This big," the twelve-year-old said, his arms spread wide apart as he could stretch them.

"No, even bigger," the younger boy said.

Cedric had been peering through the door screen but now stepped outside.

"What you boys talking about?" he asked.

"A fish," the older boy said, "in the pool below the bridge."

Rudisell, the oldest of the three at eighty-nine, expertly delivered a squirt of tobacco between himself and the boys. Creech and Campbell simply nodded at each other knowingly. Time had banished them to the role of spectators in the world's affairs, and from their perspective the world both near and far was now controlled by fools. The causes of this devolution dominated their daily conversations. The octogenarians Rudisell and Campbell blamed Franklin Roosevelt and fluoridated water. Creech, a mere seventy-six, leaned toward Elvis Presley and television.

"The biggest fish ever come out of the Tuckaseegee was a thirty-one-inch brown trout caught in nineteen and forty-eight," Rudisell announced to all present. "I seen it weighed in this very store. Fifteen pounds and two ounces."

The other men nodded in confirmation.

"This fish was twice bigger than that," the younger boy challenged.

The boy's impudence elicited another spray of tobacco juice from Rudisell.

"Must be a whale what swum up from the ocean," Creech said. "Though that's a long haul. It'd have to come up the Gulf

Coast and the Mississippi, for the water this side of the mountain flows west."

"Could be one of them log fish," Campbell offered. "They get that big. Them rascals will grab your bait and then turn into a big chunk of wood afore you can set the hook."

"They's snakes all over that pool, even some copperheads," Rudisell warned. "You younguns best go somewhere else to make up your tall tales."

The smaller boy pooched out his lower lip as if about to cry.

"Come on," his brother said. "They ain't going to believe us."

The boys walked back across the road to the bridge. The old men watched as the youths leaned over the railing, took a last look before climbing atop their bicycles and riding away.

"Fluoridated water," Rudisell wheezed. "Makes them see things."

ON THE FOLLOWING Saturday morning, Harley Wease scrambled up the same bank the boys had, carrying the remnants of his Zebco 202. Harley's hands trembled as he laid the shattered rod and reel on the ground before the old men. He pulled a soiled handkerchief from his jeans and wiped his bleeding index finger to reveal a deep slice between the first and second joints. The old men studied the finger and the rod and reel and awaited explanation. They were attentive, for Harley's deceased father had been a close friend of Rudisell's.

"Broke my rod like it was made of balsa wood," Harley said. "Then the gears on the reel got stripped. It got down to just me and the line pretty quick." Harley raised his index finger so the men could see it better. "I figured to use my finger for the drag. If the line hadn't broke, you'd be looking at a nub."

"You sure it was a fish?" Campbell asked. "Maybe you caught hold of a muskrat or snapping turkle."

"Not unless them critters has got to where they grow fins," Harley said.

"You saying it was a trout?" Creech asked.

"I only got a glimpse, but it didn't look like no trout. Looked like a alligator but for the fins."

"I never heard of no such fish in Jackson County," Campbell said, "but Rudy Nicholson's boys seen the same. It's pretty clear there's *something* in that pool."

The men turned to Rudisell for his opinion.

"I don't know what it is either," Rudisell said. "But I aim to find out."

He lifted the weathered ladder-back chair, held it aloft shakily as he made his slow way across the road to the bridge. Harley went into the store to talk with Cedric, but the other two men followed Rudisell as if all were deposed kings taking their thrones into some new kingdom. They lined their chairs up at the railing. They waited.

Only Creech had undiminished vision, but in the coming days that was rectified. Campbell had not thought anything beyond five feet of himself worth viewing for years, but now a pair of thick, round-lensed spectacles adorned his head, giving him a look of owlish intelligence. Rudisell had a spyglass he claimed once belonged to a German U-boat captain. The bridge was now effectively one lane, but traffic tended to be light. While trucks and cars drove around them, the old men kept vigil morning to evening, retreating into the store only when rain came.

Vehicles sometimes paused on the bridge to ask for updates, because the lower half of Harley Wease's broken rod had become an object of great wonder since being mounted on Cedric's back wall. Men and boys frequently took it down to grip the hard plastic handle. They invariably pointed the jagged fiberglass in the direction of the bridge, held it out as if a divining rod that might yet give some measure or resonance of what creature now made the pool its lair.

Rudisell spotted the fish first. A week had passed with daily rains clouding the river, but two days of sun settled the silt, the shallow tailrace clear all the way to the bottom. This was where Rudisell aimed his spyglass, setting it on the rail to steady his aim. He made a slow sweep of the sandy floor every fifteen minutes. Many things came into focus as he adjusted the scope: a flurry of nymphs rising to become mayflies, glints of fool's gold, schools of minnows shifting like migrating birds, crayfish with pincers raised as if surrendering to the behemoth sharing the pool with them.

It wasn't there, not for hours, but then suddenly it was. At first Rudisell saw just a shadow over the white sand, slowly gaining depth and definition, and then the slow wave of the gills and pectoral fins, the shudder of the tail as the fish held its place in the current.

"I see it," Rudisell whispered, "in the tailrace." Campbell took off his glasses and grabbed the spyglass, placed it against his best eye as Creech got up slowly, leaned over the rail.

"It's long as my leg," Creech said.

"I never thought to see such a thing," Campbell uttered.

The fish held its position a few more moments before slowly moving into deeper water.

"I never seen the like of a fish like that," Creech announced.

"It ain't a trout," Campbell said.

"Nor carp or bass," Rudisell added.

"Maybe it is a gator," Campbell said. "One of them snowbirds from Florida could of put it in there."

"No," Rudisell said. "I seen gators during my army training in Louisiana. A gator's like us, it's got to breathe air. This thing don't need air. Beside, it had a tail fin."

"Maybe it's a mermaid," Creech mused.

By late afternoon the bridge looked like an overloaded barge. Pickups, cars, and two tractors clotted both sides of the road and the store's parking lot. Men and boys squirmed and shifted to get a place against the railing. Harley Wease recounted his epic battle, but it was the ancients who were most deferred to as they made pronouncements about size and weight. Of species they could speak only by negation.

"My brother works down at that nuclear power plant near Walhalla," Marcus Price said. "Billy swears there's catfish below the dam near five foot long. Claims that radiation makes them bigger."

"This ain't no catfish," Rudisell said. "It didn't have no big jug head. More lean than that."

Bascombe Greene ventured the shape called to mind the pike-fish caught in weedy lakes up north. Stokes Hamilton thought it could be a hellbender salamander, for though he'd never seen one more than twelve inches long he'd heard tell they got to six feet in Japan. Leonard Coffey told a long, convoluted story about a goldfish set free in a pond. After two decades of being fed corn bread and fried okra, the fish had been caught and it weighed fifty-seven pounds.

"It ain't no pike nor spring lizard nor goldfish," Rudisell said emphatically.

"Well, there's but one way to know," Bascombe Greene said, "and that's to try and catch the damn thing." Bascombe nodded at Harley. "What bait was you fishing with?"

Harley looked sheepish.

"I'd lost my last spinner when I snagged a limb. All I had left in my tackle box was a rubber worm I use for bass, so I put it on."

"What size and color?" Bascombe asked. "We got to be scientific about this."

"Seven inch," Harley said. "It was purple with white dots."

"You got any more of them?" Leonard Coffey asked.

"No, but you can buy them at Sylva Hardware."

"Won't do you no good," Rudisell said.

"Why not?" Leonard asked.

"For a fish to live long enough to get that big, it's got to be smart. It'll not forget that a rubber worm tricked it."

"It might not be near smart as you reckon," Bascombe said. "I don't mean no disrespect, but old folks tend to be forgetful. Maybe that old fish is the same way."

"I reckon we'll know the truth of that soon enough," Rudisell concluded, because fishermen already cast from the bridge and banks. Soon several lines had gotten tangled, and a fistfight broke out over who had claim to a choice spot near the pool's tailrace. More people arrived as the afternoon wore on, became early evening. Cedric, never one to miss a potential business opportunity, put a plastic fireman's hat on his head and a whistle in his mouth. He parked cars while his son Bobby crossed and recrossed the bridge selling Cokes from a battered shopping cart.

Among the later arrivals was Charles Meekins, the county's game warden. He was thirty-eight years old and had grown up in Madison, Wisconsin. The general consensus, especially among the old men, was the warden was arrogant and a smart-ass. Meekins stopped often at the store, and he invariably addressed them as Wynken, Blynken, and Nod. He listened with undisguised condescension as the old men, Harley, and finally the two boys told of what they'd seen.

"It's a trout or carp," Meekins said, "carp" sounding like "cop." Despite four years in Jackson County, Meekins still spoke as if his vocal cords had been pulled from his throat and reinstalled in his sinus cavity. "There's no fish larger in these waters."

Harley handed his reel to the game warden.

"That fish stripped the gears on it."

Meekins inspected the reel as he might an obviously fraudulent fishing license.

"You probably didn't have the drag set right."

"It was bigger than any trout or carp," Campbell insisted.

"When you're looking into water you can't really judge the size of something," Meekins said. He looked at some of the younger men and winked. "Especially if your vision isn't all that good to begin with."

A palmful of Red Mule chewing tobacco bulged the right side of Rudisell's jaw like a tumor, but his apoplexy was such that he swallowed a portion of his cud and began hacking violently.

Campbell slapped him on the back and Rudisell spewed dark bits of tobacco onto the bridge's wooden flooring.

Meekins had gotten back in his green fish and wildlife truck before Rudisell recovered enough to speak.

"If I hadn't near choked to death I'd have told that shitbritches youngun to bend over and we'd see if my sight was good enough to ram this spyglass up his ass."

IN THE NEXT few days so many fishermen came to try their luck that Rudisell finally bought a wire-bound notebook from Cedric and had anglers sign up for fifteen-minute slots. They cast almost every offering imaginable into the pool. A good half of the anglers succumbed to the theory that what had worked before could work again, so rubber worms were the single most popular choice. The rubber-worm devotees used an array of different sizes, hues, and even smells. Some went with seven-inch rubber worms while others favored five- or ten-inch. Some tried purple worms with white dots while others tried white with purple dots and still others tried pure white and pure black and every variation between including chartreuse, pink, turquoise, and fuchsia. Some used rubber worms with auger tails and others used flat tails. Some worms smelled like motor oil and some worms smelled like strawberries and some worms had no smell at all.

The others were divided by their devotion to live bait or artificial lures. Almost all the bait fishermen used night crawlers and red worms in the belief that if the fish had been fooled by an imitation, the actual live worm would work even better, but they also cast spring lizards, minnows, crickets, grubs, wasp larvae, crawfish, frogs, newts, toads, and even a live field mouse. The lure contingent favored spinners of the Panther Martin and Roostertail variety though they were not averse to Rapalas, Jitterbugs, Hula Poppers, Johnson Silver Minnows, Devilhorses, and a dozen other hook-laden pieces of wood or plastic. Some lures sank and bounced along the bottom and some lures floated and still others gurgled and rattled and some made no sound at all and one lure even changed colors depending on depth and water temperature. Jarvis Hampton cast a Rapala F 14 he'd once caught a tarpon with in Florida. A subgroup of fly fishermen cast Muddler Minnows, Woolly Boogers, Woolly Worms, Royal Coachmen, streamers and wet flies, nymphs and dry flies, and some hurled nymphs and dry flies together that swung overhead like miniature bolas.

During the first two days five brown trout, one speckled trout, one ball cap, two smallmouth bass, ten knotty heads, a bluegill, and one old boot were caught. A gray squirrel was snagged by an errant cast into a tree. Neither the squirrel nor the various fish outweighed the boot, which weighed one pound and eight ounces after the water was poured out. On the third day Wesley McIntire's rod doubled and the drag whirred. A rainbow trout leaped in the pool's center, Wesley's quarter-ounce Panther Martin spinner embedded in its upper jaw. He fought the trout for five minutes before his brother Robbie could net it. The rainbow was twenty-two inches long and weighed five and a half pounds, big enough that Wesley took it straight to the taxidermist to be mounted.

Charles Meekins came by an hour later. He didn't get out of the truck, just rolled down his window and nodded. His radio

played loudly and the atonal guitars and screeching voices made
Rudisell glad he was mostly deaf, because hearing only part of the
racket made him feel like stinging wasps swarmed inside his head.
Meekins didn't bother to turn the radio down, just shouted over
the music.

"I told you it was a trout."

"That wasn't it," Rudisell shouted. "The fish I seen could of
eaten that rainbow for breakfast."

Meekins smiled, showing a set of bright white teeth that, unlike Rudisell's, did not have to be deposited in a glass jar every
night.

"Then why didn't it? That rainbow has probably been in that
pool for years." Meekins shook his head. "I wish you old boys
would learn to admit when you're wrong about something."

Meekins rolled up his window as Rudisell pursed his lips and
fired a stream of tobacco juice directly at the warden's left eye.
The tobacco hit the glass and dribbled a dark, phlegmy rivulet
down the window.

"A fellow such as that ought not be allowed a guvment uniform," Creech said.

"Not unless it's got black and white stripes all up and down
it," Crenshaw added.

After ten days no other fish of consequence had been caught
and anglers began giving up. The notebook was discarded because
appointments were no longer necessary. Meekins's belief gained
credence, especially since in ten days none of the hundred or so
men and boys who'd gathered there had seen the giant fish.

"I'd be hunkered down on the stream bottom too if such
commotion was going on around me," Creech argued, but few

remained to nod in agreement. Even Harley Wease began to have doubts.

"Maybe that rainbow *was* what I had on," he said heretically.

BY THE FIRST week in May only the old men remained on the bridge. They kept their vigil but the occupants of cars and trucks and tractors no longer paused to ask about sightings. When the fish reappeared in the tailrace, the passing drivers ignored the old men's frantic waves to come see. They drove across the bridge with eyes fixed straight ahead, embarrassed by their elders' dementia.

"That's the best look we've gotten yet," Campbell said when the fish moved out of the shallows and into deeper water. "It's six feet long if it's a inch."

Rudisell set his spyglass on the bridge railing and turned to Creech, the one among them who still had a car and driver's license.

"You got to drive me over to Jarvis Hampton's house," Rudisell said.

"What for?" Creech asked.

"Because we're going to rent out that rod and reel he uses for them tarpon. Then we got to go by the library, because I want to know what this thing is when we catch it."

Creech kept the speedometer at a steady thirty-five as they followed the river south to Jarvis Hampton's farm. They found Jarvis in his tobacco field and quickly negotiated a ten-dollar-a-week rental for the rod and reel, four 2/0 vanadium-steel fishhooks, and four sinkers. Jarvis offered a net as well but Rudisell claimed it wasn't big enough for what they were after. "But I'll take a hay hook and a whetstone if you got it," Rudisell added, "and some bailing twine and a feed sack."

They packed the fishing equipment in the trunk and drove to the county library, where they used Campbell's library card to check out an immense tome called *Freshwater Fish of North America*. The book was so heavy that only Creech had the strength to carry it, holding it before him with both hands as if it were made of stone. He dropped it in the backseat and, still breathing heavily, got behind the wheel and cranked the engine.

"We got one more stop," Rudisell said, "that old millpond on Spillcorn Creek."

"You wanting to practice with that rod and reel?" Campbell asked.

"No, to get our bait," Rudisell replied. "I been thinking about something. After that fish hit Harley's rubber worm they was throwing night crawlers right and left into the pool figuring that fish thought Harley's lure was a worm. But what if it thought that rubber worm was something else, something we ain't seen one time since we been watching the pool though it used to be thick with them?"

Campbell understood first.

"I get what you're saying, but this is one bait I'd rather not be gathering myself, or putting on a hook for that matter."

"Well, if you'll just hold the sack I'll do the rest."

"What about baiting the hook?"

"I'll do that too."

Since the day was warm and sunny, a number of reptiles had gathered on the stone slabs that had once been a dam. Most were blue-tailed skinks and fence lizards, but several mud-colored serpents coiled sullenly on the largest stones. Creech, who was deathly afraid of snakes, remained in the car. Campbell carried the burlap feed sack, reluctantly trailing Rudisell through broom sedge to the old dam.

"Them snakes ain't of the poisonous persuasion?" Campbell asked.

Rudisell turned and shook his head.

"Naw. Them's just your common water snake. Mean as the devil but they got no fangs."

As they got close the skinks and lizards darted for crevices in the rocks, but the snakes did not move until Rudisell's shadow fell over them. Three slithered away before Rudisell's creaky back could bend enough for him to grab hold, but the fourth did not move until Rudisell's liver-spotted hand closed around its neck. The snake thrashed violently, its mouth biting at the air. Campbell reluctantly moved closer, his fingers and thumbs holding the sack open, arms extended out from his body as if attempting to catch some object falling from the sky. As soon as Rudisell dropped the serpent in, Campbell gave the snake and sack to Rudisell, who knotted the burlap and put it in the trunk.

"You figure one to be enough?" Campbell asked.

"Yes," Rudisell replied. "We'll get but one chance."

The sun was beginning to settle over Balsam Mountain when the old men got back to the bridge. Rudisell led them down the path to the riverbank, the feed sack in his right hand, the hay hook and twine in his left. Campbell came next with the rod and reel and sinkers and hooks. Creech came last, the great book clutched to his chest. The trail became steep and narrow, the weave of leaf and limb overhead so thick it seemed they were entering a cave.

Once they got to the bank and caught their breath, they went to work. Creech used two of the last teeth left in his head to clamp three sinkers onto the line, then tied the hook to the monofilament with an expertly rendered hangman's knot. Campbell studied the book and found the section on fish living in southeastern rivers. He folded the page where the photographs of relevant species began and then marked the back section where corresponding printed information was located. Rudisell took out the whetstone and sharpened the metal with the same attentiveness as the long-ago warriors who once roamed these hills had honed their weapons, those bronze men who'd flaked dull stone to make their flesh-piercing arrowheads. Soon the steel tip shone like silver.

"All right, I done my part," Creech said when he'd tested the drag. He eyed the writhing feed sack apprehensively. "I ain't about to be close by when you try to get that snake on a hook."

Creech moved over near the tailwaters as Campbell picked up the rod and reel. He settled the rod tip above Rudisell's head, the fishhook dangling inches from the older man's beaky nose. Rudisell unknotted the sack, then pinched the fishhook's eye between his left hand's index finger and thumb, used the right to slowly peel back the burlap. When the snake was exposed, Rudisell grabbed it by the neck, stuck the fishhook through the midsection, and quickly let go. The rod tip sagged with the snake's weight as Creech moved farther down the bank.

"What do I do now?" Campbell shouted, for the snake was swinging in an arc that brought the serpent ever closer to his body.

"Cast it," Rudisell replied.

Campbell made a frantic sideways, two-handed heave that

looked more like someone throwing a tub of dishwater off a back porch than a cast. The snake landed three feet from the bank, but luck was with them for it began swimming underwater toward the pool's center. Creech came back to stand by Campbell, but his eyes nervously watched the line. He flexed his arthritic right knee like a runner at the starting line, ready to flee up the bank if the snake took a mind to change direction. Rudisell gripped the hay hook's handle in his right hand. With his left he began wrapping bailing twine around metal and flesh. The wooden bridge floor rumbled like low thunder as a pickup crossed. A few seconds later another vehicle passed over the bridge. Rudisell continued wrapping the twine. He had no watch but suspected it was after five and men working in Sylva were starting to come home. When Rudisell had used up all the twine, Creech knotted it.

"With that hay hook tied to you it looks like you're the bait," Creech joked.

"If I gaff that thing it's not going to get free of me," Rudisell vowed.

The snake was past the deepest part of the pool now, making steady progress toward the far bank. It struggled to the surface briefly, the weight of the sinkers pulling it back down. The line remained motionless for a few moments, then began a slow movement back toward the heart of the pool.

"Why you figure it to turn around?" Campbell asked as Creech took a first step farther up the bank.

"I don't know," Rudisell said. "Why don't you tighten your line a bit."

Campbell turned the handle twice and the monofilament grew taut and the rod tip bent. "Damn snake's got hung up."

"Give it a good jerk and it'll come free," Creech said. "Probably just tangled in some brush."

Campbell yanked upward, and the rod bowed. The line began moving upstream, not fast but steady, the reel chattering as the monofilament stripped off.

"It's on," Campbell said softly, as if afraid to startle the fish.

The line did not pause until it was thirty yards upstream and in the shadow of the bridge.

"You got to turn it," Rudisell shouted, "or it'll wrap that line around one of them pillars."

"Turn it," Campbell replied. "I can't even slow it down."

But the fish turned of its own volition, headed back into the deeper water. For fifteen minutes the creature sulked on the pool's bottom. Campbell kept the rod bowed, breathing hard as he strained against the immense weight on the other end. Finally, the fish began moving again, over to the far bank and then upstream. Campbell's arms trembled violently.

"My arms is give out," he said and handed the rod to Creech. Campbell sprawled out on the bank, his chest heaving rapidly, limbs shaking as if palsied. The fish swam back into the pool's heart and another ten minutes passed. Rudisell looked up at the bridge. Cars and trucks continued to rumble across. Several vehicles paused a few moments but no faces appeared at the railing.

Creech tightened the drag and the rod bent double.

"Easy," Rudisell said. "You don't want him breaking off."

"The way it's going, it'll kill us all before it gets tired," Creech gasped.

The additional pressure worked. The fish moved again, this

time allowing the line in its mouth to lead it into the tailrace. For the first time they saw the behemoth.

"Lord amercy," Campbell exclaimed, for what they saw was over six feet long and enclosed in a brown suit of prehistoric armor, the immense tail curved like a scythe. When the fish saw the old men it surged away, the drag chattering again as the creature moved back into the deeper water.

Rudisell sat down beside the book and rapidly turned pages of color photos until he saw it.

"It's a sturgeon," he shouted, then turned to where the printed information was and began to call out bursts of information. "Can grow over seven feet long and three hundred pounds. That stuff that looks like armor is called scutes. They's even got a Latin name here. Says it was once in near every river, but now endangered. Can live a hundred and fifty years."

"I ain't going to live another hundred and fifty seconds if I don't get some relief," Creech said and handed the rod back to Campbell.

Campbell took over as Creech collapsed on the bank. The sturgeon began to give ground, the reel handle making slow, clockwise revolutions.

Rudisell closed the book and stepped into the shallows of the pool's tailrace. A sandbar formed a few yards out and that was what he moved toward, the hay hook raised like a metal question mark. Once he'd secured himself on the sandbar, Rudisell turned to Campbell.

"Lead him over here. There's no way we can lift him up the bank."

"You gonna try to gill that thing?" Creech asked incredulously.

Rudisell shook his head.

"I ain't gonna gill it, I'm going to stab this hay hook in so deep it'll have to drag me back into that pool as well to get away."

The reel handle turned quicker now, and soon the sturgeon came out of the depths, emerging like a submarine. Campbell moved farther down the bank, only three or four yards from the sandbar. Creech got up and stood beside Campbell. The fish swam straight toward them, face-first, as if led on a leash. They could see the head clearly now, the cone-shaped snout, barbels hanging beneath the snout like whiskers. As it came closer Rudisell creakily kneeled down on the sandbar's edge. As he swung the hay hook the sturgeon made a last surge toward deeper water. The bright metal raked across the scaly back but did not penetrate.

"Damn," Rudisell swore.

"You got to beach it," Creech shouted at Campbell, who began reeling again, not pausing until the immense head was half out of the water, snout touching the sandbar. The sturgeon's wide mouth opened, revealing an array of rusting hooks and lures that hung from the lips like medals.

"Gaff it now," Creech shouted.

"Hurry," Campbell huffed, the rod in his hands doubled like a bow. "I'm herniating myself."

But Rudisell appeared not to hear them. He stared intently at the fish, the hay hook held overhead as if it were a torch allowing him to see the sturgeon more clearly.

Rudisell's blue eyes brightened for a moment, and an enigmatic smile creased his face. The hay hook's sharpened point flashed, aimed not at the fish but at the monofilament. A loud twang like a broken guitar string sounded across the water. The rod whipped back and Campbell stumbled backward, but Creech caught him before he fell. The sturgeon was motionless for a few moments, then slowly curved back toward the pool's heart. As it disappeared, Rudisell remained kneeling on the sandbar, his eyes gazing into the pool. Campbell and Creech staggered over to the bank and sat down.

"They'll never believe us," Creech said, "not in a million years, especially that smart-ass game warden."

"We had it good as caught," Campbell muttered. "We had it caught."

None of them spoke further for a long while, all exhausted by the battle. But their silence had more to do with each man's reflection on what he had just witnessed than with weariness. A yellow mayfly rose like a watery spark in the tailrace, hung in the air a few moments before it fell and was swept away by the current. As time passed crickets announced their presence on the bank, and downriver a whippoorwill called. More mayflies rose in the tailrace. The air became chilly as the sheltering trees closed more tightly around them, absorbed the waning sun's light, a preamble to another overdue darkness.

"It's okay," Campbell finally said.

Creech looked at Rudisell, who was still on the sandbar.

"You done the right thing. I didn't see that at first, but I see it now."

Rudisell finally stood up, wiped the wet sand from the knees of his pants. As he stepped into the shallows he saw something in the water. He picked it up and put it in his pocket.

"Find you a fleck of gold?" Campbell asked.

"Better than gold," Rudisell replied and joined his comrades on the bank.

THEY COULD HARDLY see their own feet as they walked up the path to the bridge. When they emerged, they found the green fish and wildlife truck parked at the trail end. The passenger window was down and Meekins's smug face looked out at them.

"So you old boys haven't drowned after all. Folks saw the empty chairs and figured you'd fallen in."

Meekins nodded at the fishing equipment in Campbell's hands and smiled.

"Have any luck catching your monster?"

"Caught it and let it go," Campbell said.

"That's mighty convenient," Meekins said. "I don't suppose anyone else actually saw this giant fish, or that you have a photograph."

"No," Creech said serenely. "But it's way bigger than you are."

Meekins shook his head. He no longer smiled. "Must be nice to have nothing better to do than make up stories, but this is getting old real quick."

Rudisell stepped up to the truck's window, only inches away from Meekins's face when he raised his hand. A single diamond-shaped object was wedged between Rudisell's gnarled index finger and thumb. Though tinted brown, it appeared to be translucent. He held it eye level in front of Meekins's face as if it were a silty monocle they both might peer through.

"*Acipenser fulvescens,*" Rudisell said, the Latin uttered slowly as if an incantation. He put the scute back in his pocket and, without further acknowledgment of Meekins's existence, stepped around the truck and onto the hardtop. Campbell followed with the fishing equipment and Creech came last with the book. It was a slow, dignified procession. They walked westward toward the store, the late-afternoon sun burnishing their cracked and wasted faces. Coming out of the shadows, they blinked their eyes as if dazzled, much in the manner of old-world saints who have witnessed the blinding brilliance of the one true vision.

❖

Chemistry

The spring my father spent three weeks at Broughton Hospital, he came back to my mother and me pale and disoriented, two pill bottles clutched in his right hand as we made our awkward reunion in the hospital lobby. A portly, gray-haired man wearing a tie and tweed jacket soon joined us. Dr. Morris pronounced my father "greatly improved, well on his way to recovery," but even in those first few minutes my mother and I were less sure. My father seemed to be in a holding pattern, not the humorous, confident man he had been before his life swerved to some bleak reckoning, but also not the man who'd lain in bed those April mornings when my mother called the high school to arrange for a substitute. He now seemed like a shipwreck survivor, treading water but unable to swim.

"All he needs is a hobby," Dr. Morris said, patting my father's back as if they were old friends, "to keep his mind off his mind." The doctor laughed and straightened his tie, added as if an afterthought, "and the medicine, of course." Dr. Morris patted my father's back again. "A chemistry teacher knows how important that is."

My father took half of Dr. Morris's advice. As soon as we got home, he brought the steel oxygen tank clanging down from the attic and gathered the wet suit, mask, and flippers he hadn't worn since his navy days. He put it all on to check for leaks and rips, his webbed feet flapping as he moved around the living room like some half-evolved creature.

"I'm not sure this was the kind of hobby Dr. Morris had in mind," my mother said, trying to catch the eyes behind the mask. "It seems dangerous."

My father did not reply. He was testing the mouthpiece while adjusting the straps that held the air tanks. That done, he made swimming motions with his arms as he raised his knees toward his chest like a drum major.

"I've got some repairs to make," he said, and flapped on out to the garage. While my mother cooked a homecoming supper of pork chops and rice, he prepared himself to enter the deep gloaming of channels and drop-offs with thirty minutes of breath strapped to his back.

My father still wore his wet suit and fins when he sat down at the supper table that evening. He ate everything on his plate, which heartened my mother and me, and drank glass after glass of iced tea as if possessed by an unquenchable thirst. But when he lay his napkin on the table, he did not refill his glass with more tea and reach for the pill bottles my mother had placed beside his plate.

"You've got to take the medicine," my mother urged. "It's going to heal you."

"Heal me," my father mused. "You sound like Dr. Morris. He said the same thing right before they did the shock treatments."

My mother looked at her plate.

"Can't you see that's exactly why you need to take the pills? So you won't ever have to do that again." She raised her napkin to blot a tear from her cheek, her voice a mere whisper now. "This is not something to be ashamed of, Paul. It's no different from taking penicillin for an infection."

But my father was adamant. He pushed the tinted bottles to the center of the table one at a time as if they were chess pieces.

"How can I teach chemistry if I'm so muddled I can't find the classroom?" he said.

That spring my allegiances were with my mother, who anchored our family in ways I had not appreciated until my father lost his moorings. The following Monday my father resumed teaching, and I was her confederate at school. Between bells I peeked into a classroom filled with Styrofoam carbons and atoms wired together like fragile solar systems. In March Mr. Keller, the vice principal, had found my father crouched and sobbing in the chemical storage room, a molecular model of oxygen clutched in his hands, so it was with relief in those last weeks of my junior year that I found my father manning his desk between breaks, braced and ready for the next wave of students.

One morning he was looking up when my halved face appeared at his door. He saluted me sharply.

"Petty Officer Hampton reports no men overboard, sir," he said to me.

"Well, at least he's got his sense of humor back," my mother said when I reported the incident.

IN MID-JUNE MY father announced at Sunday breakfast he was no longer a Presbyterian. Instead of sitting with us on the polished-oak pews of Cliffside Presbyterian, he would be driving up to Cleveland County's mountainous northern corner to attend a Pentecostal church.

"It's something I've got to do," he said.

My mother laid her napkin on the table, looked at my father as if he'd just informed us he was defecting to Cuba.

"We need to talk, Paul," she said. "Alone."

My parents disappeared behind a closed bedroom door. I could hear my father's voice, moderate and reassuring, or at least attempting to be. My mother's voice, in contrast, was tense and troubled. They talked an hour, then dressed for church. I was unsure who'd prevailed until my father came out of the bedroom wearing not a suit but a shirt and tie. He cranked our decade-old Ford Fairlane and headed north into the mountains, as he would Sunday mornings and Wednesday nights for the rest of his life. Meanwhile, my mother and I drove our newer Buick Le Sabre in the opposite direction, down toward Broad River to Cliffside Presbyterian.

I was not made privy to what kind of understanding, if any, my parents had reached about my father's change in church affiliation, but it was obvious as well as inevitable that my mother found this religious transmutation troubling. A lifelong Presbyterian,

she distrusted religious fervor, especially for a man in such a tenuous mental state, but I suspect she also felt something akin to
betrayal—a rejection of much of the life his marriage to her had
made possible.

My mother had been baptized in Cliffside Presbyterian
church, but my father, who'd grown up in the high mountains of
Watauga County, had been Pentecostal before their marriage. His
conversion signaled a social as well as religious transformation, a
sign of upward mobility from hardscrabble Appalachian begin-
nings, for in this Scots-Irish community where Episcopalians were
rare as Eskimos, he worshiped with the Brahmins of the county's
Protestant hierarchy.

My father had appeared a dutiful convert, teaching Sunday
school, helping prepare the men's breakfasts, even serving a term
as an elder, but he'd been a subversive convert as well. On Sunday
mornings he entertained me with caustic remarks about the pro-
priety of the services and Presbyterians' inability to sing anything
remotely resembling a "joyful noise." When the choir rose to
sing, my father winked at me, pretended to stuff plugs in his ears.
My mother looked straight ahead at such times, trying to ignore
my father's shenanigans, but her lips always tightened.

"That wafer might as well be a burnt marshmallow for all the
passion it evokes in that crowd," my father said one Sunday as we
drove home. "If Jesus Christ and his disciples marched in during a
service, the ushers would tell them to have a seat, that the congregation would be glad to hear what they had to say as soon as the
monthly business meeting was over."

My mother glared at my father but addressed her words to the
backseat, where I sat.

"Just because a service is orderly and dignified doesn't mean it isn't heartfelt," she said. "Don't trust people who make a spectacle of what they believe, Joel. Too often it's just a show, a way of drawing attention to themselves."

AS WE ENTERED summer, our lives took on a guarded normality. My father taught a six-week summer school session. My mother resumed, after a two-month absence, her part-time job as a book-keeper for my uncle Brad's construction firm. I worked for my uncle as well, driving nails and pouring concrete. My uncle also gave us free rein of the lake house he'd bought years earlier, when he'd had the time to use it, so on Saturday mornings we drove up Highway Ten to spend the day at South Mountain Reservoir, where cool mountain breezes and teeth-chattering water might revive us after a week of wilting piedmont humidity. No doubt my mother packed up food and swimsuits each Saturday in hopes the lake might be beneficial for my father after a week of remedial teaching in an unairconditioned classroom.

My father was eager that I share his new hobby. He gave me demonstrations on how to use the scuba apparatus. At supper he spoke excitedly of water's other side. He often wore his diving equipment around the house, once opening the door to a startled paperboy while wearing a mask and fins. My mother was reluctant to let me participate, but she acquiesced when I promised not to go into the reservoir's deep heart, where a diver had drowned the previous summer. So on Saturday afternoons she read paperbacks on the screened porch and cast nervous glances toward the lake as my father and I shared the diving equipment. When my turn came, I fell backward off the dock and into the lake, watching a rushing away sky as I hit the water and sank, air bubbles rising above my head like thoughts in a comic strip.

I could never see more than a few yards, but that was enough. Arm-long catfish swam into view sudden as a nightmare, their blunt, whiskered faces rooting the bottom. Loggerheads big as hubcaps walked the lake floor, their hand-grenade heads ready to bite off a careless finger. I found what no longer lived down there as well: fish suspended like kites, monofilament trailing from their mouths to line-wrapped snags below; drowned litters of kittens and puppies; once an out-of-season deer, a gash on its head where the antlers had been. On the reservoir's floor even the familiar startled. Gaudy bass plugs hung on limbs and stumps like Christmas ornaments; branches snapped off like black icicles; a refrigerator yawned open like an unsprung trap.

Each time I entered the water my foreboding increased, not chest-tightening panic but a growing certainty that many things in the world were better left hidden. By August I'd joined my mother on the porch, playing board games and drinking iced tea as my father disappeared off the dock toward mysteries I no longer wished to fathom.

On one of these August afternoons after he'd finished diving, my father decided to drive out to the highway and buy ice so we could churn ice cream. "Come with me, Joel," he said. "I might need some help."

Once we turned onto the blacktop, my father passed two convenience stores before pulling in to what had once been a gas station. Now only a weedy cement island remained, the pumps long uprooted. HOLCOMBE'S STORE, nothing more, appeared on a rusting black-and-white sign above the door. REDWORMS AND MINNERS FOR SALE was scrawled eye level on a second sign made of cardboard.

We stepped inside, adjusting our eyes to what little light filtered through the dusty windows. A radio played gospel music. Canned goods and paper plates, toilet paper and boxes of cereal lined the shelves. A man about my father's age sat behind the counter, black hair combed slick across his scalp, a mole above his right eyebrow the size and color of a tarnished penny. The man stood up from his chair and smiled, his two front teeth chipped and discolored.

"Why, hi, Brother Hampton," he said warmly in a thick mountain accent. "What brings you up this way?"

"Spending Saturday on the lake," my father said, then nodded toward me. "This is my son Joel."

"Carl Holcombe," the man said, extending his hand. I felt the calluses on his palm, the wedding ring worn on his right hand.

"We're going to make ice cream," my father said. "I was hoping you had some ice."

"Wish I could help you but I weren't selling enough to keep the truck coming by," Mr. Holcombe said.

"How about some worms then?"

"That I can help you with." Mr. Holcombe came around the counter, walking with a slight limp as he made his way to the back of the store.

"How many boxes?" he asked, opening a refrigerator.

"Four," my father said.

My father laid a five-dollar bill on the counter. Mr. Holcombe rang up the sale.

"See you at church tomorrow?" Mr. Holcombe asked, dropping coins into my father's hand. My father nodded.

I tried not to stare at the mole as Mr. Holcombe filled my hands with the cardboard containers.

"Your daddy," he said to me, "is a Godly man, but I suspect you already know that."

He closed the cash register and walked with us to the entrance.

"I hope you all catch something," he said, holding the tattered screen door open.

"Why did you buy the worms?" I asked my father as we drove off.

"Because he needs the money," my father said. "We'll let them go in the garden."

"Mr. Holcombe's a friend of yours?" I asked, wondering if my father would note the surprise in my voice.

"Yes," my father said. "He's also my pastor."

THE FOLLOWING WEDNESDAY my father left to attend his midweek church service. I'd already asked my mother if I could borrow the Buick that evening, so when he departed so did I, following the Fairlane through town. At the stoplight I too turned right onto Highway Ten. Since the previous Saturday I'd been perplexed about what could compel my father, a man with a university education, to drive a good half hour to hear a preacher who, if his spelling and grammar were any indication, probably hadn't finished high school.

Outside of town it began to rain. I turned on the Buick's windshield wipers and headlights. Soon hills became mountains, red clay darkened to black dirt. I swallowed to relieve the ear pressure from the change in altitude as the last ranch-style brick house, the last broad, manicured lawn, vanished from my rearview mirror. Stands of oaks and dogwoods crowded the roadsides. Gaps in the woods revealed the green rise of corn and tobacco, pastures framed by rusty barbed-wire fences. Occasionally I passed a prosperous look-ing two-story farmhouse, but most homes were trailers or four-room A-frames, often with pickups, cars, and appliances rusting in the side yards, scrawny beagles and blueticks chained under trees.

The rain quit so I cut off the windshield wipers, let the Fair-lane get farther ahead of me. I came over a rise and the Fairlane had already disappeared around a curve. I sped up, afraid I'd lost my father, but coming out of the curve I saw his car stopped in the road a hundred yards ahead, the turn signal on though our Buick was the closest car behind him. My father turned onto a dirt road and I followed, still keeping my distance though I wondered if it were really necessary. He slowed in front of a cinder-block build-ing no bigger than a woodshed, pulling into a makeshift parking lot where our ancient Fairlane looked no older than the dozen other cars and trucks. I eased off the road on a rise above the church and watched my father walk hurriedly toward the build-ing. A white cross was nailed above the door he entered.

I could hear an out-of-tune piano, a chorus of voices rising from the open door and windows into the August evening, merg-ing with the songs of crickets and cicadas. I waited half an hour before I got out of the Buick and walked down the road to the church. At the front door I paused, then stepped into a foyer small and dark as a closet. A half-open door led to the main room. The singing stopped, replaced by a single voice.

I peered into a thick-shadowed room whose only light came from a single bare bulb dangling from the ceiling. Mr. Holcombe stood in front of three rows of metal chairs where the congregation sat. At his feet lay a wooden box that looked like an infant's coffin. Holes had been bored in its lid. Mr. Holcombe wore no coat or tie, just a white, short-sleeved shirt, brown slacks, and scuffed black loafers. His arm outstretched, he waved a Bible as if fanning an invisible flame.

"The word of the Lord," he said, then opened the Bible to a page marked by a paper scrap. "And they cast out many devils, and anointed with oil many that were sick, and healed them," Mr. Holcombe read. He closed the Bible and went down on one knee in front of the wooden box, his head bowed, like an athlete resting on the sidelines.

"Whoever is afflicted, come forward," he said. "Lord, if it is your will, let us be the instrument of thy healing grace."

"Amen," the congregation said as my father left the last row and kneeled beside Mr. Holcombe. Without a word the congregation rose and gathered around my father. An old woman, gray hair reaching her hips, opened a bottle and dabbed a thick, clear liquid on my father's brow. The other members laid their hands on his head and shoulders.

"Oh, Lord," shouted Mr. Holcombe, raising the Bible in his hand. "Grant this child of God continued victories over his affliction. Let not his heart be troubled. Let him know your abiding presence."

The old woman with the long hair began speaking feverishly in a language I couldn't understand, her hands straining upward as if she were attempting to haul heaven down into their midst.

"Praise God, praise God," a man in a plaid shirt shouted as he did a spastic dance around the others.

My father began speaking the strange, fervent language of the old woman. The congregation removed their hands as my father rocked his torso back and forth, sounds I could not translate pouring from his mouth.

Mr. Holcombe, still kneeling beside my father, unclasped the wooden box. The room suddenly became silent, then a whirring sound like a dry gourd being shaken. At first I did not realize where the noise came from, but when Mr. Holcombe dipped his hand and forearm into the box the sound increased. Something was in there, something alive and, I knew even before seeing it, dangerous.

Mr. Holcombe's forearm rose out of the box, a timber rattlesnake coiled around his wrist like a thick, black vine. The reptile's head rose inches above Mr. Holcombe's open palm, its split tongue probing the air like a sensor.

I turned away, stepped out of the foyer and into the parking lot. My eyes slowly adjusted to being outside the church's dense shadows. I stood there until the scraping of chairs signaled the congregation's return to their seats. They sang a hymn, and then Mr. Holcombe slowly read a long passage from the book of Mark.

I walked back to the Buick, halfway there when I saw the headlights were on. I tried the battery five times and gave up, dragging the jumper cables from the trunk and opening the hood in the hope someone might stop and help me. No cars or trucks passed, however, and in a few minutes people came out of the church, some pausing to speak but most going straight to their vehicles. I sat in the car and waited until I saw our Fairlane leave the parking lot.

My father pulled off the road in front of the Buick, hood to hood, as though he already knew the problem. I stepped out of the car.

"What happened?" he asked.

I wasn't sure how to answer his question, but I gave the simplest answer.

"The battery's dead," I said, holding up the jumper cables as if to validate my words.

He opened the Fairlane's hood. We clamped the cables to the batteries, then got back in and cranked the engines. My father unhooked the cables and came around to the Buick's passenger side. He dropped the jumper cables on the floorboard and sat down beside me. Both engines were running, the cars aimed at each other like a wreck about to happen.

"Why did you follow me?" my father asked, looking out the window. There was no anger in his voice, just curiosity.

"To find out why you come here."

"Do you know now?"

"No."

The last two cars left the church. The drivers slowed as they passed, but my father waved them on.

"Dr. Morris says I've got too much salt in my brain, a chemical imbalance," my father said. "It's an easy problem for him with an easy solution, so many milligrams of Elavil, so many volts of electricity. But I can't believe it's that simple."

Perhaps it was the hum of the engines, my father looking out the window as he spoke, but I felt as if we were traveling although the landscape did not change. It was like I could feel the earth's slow revolution as August's strange, pink glow tinted the evening's last light.

My father shut his eyes for a moment. He'd aged in the last year, his hair gray at the edges, his brow lined.

"Your mother believes the holy rollers got me too young, that they raised me to see the world only the way they see it. But she's wrong about that. There was a time I could understand everything from a single atom to the whole universe with a blackboard and a piece of chalk, and it was beautiful as any hymn the way it all came together."

My father nodded toward the church, barely visible now in the gloaming.

"You met Carl Holcombe. His wife and five-year-old daughter got killed eleven years ago in a car wreck, a wreck that was Carl's fault because he was driving too fast. Carl says there are whole weeks he can't remember he was so drunk, nights he put a gun barrel under his chin and held it there an hour. There was nothing in this world to sustain him, so he had to look somewhere else. I've had to do the same."

Though the cars still idled, we sat there in silence a few more minutes, long enough to see the night's first fireflies sparking like matches in the woods. My father's face was submerged in shadows when he spoke again.

"What I'm trying to say is that some solutions aren't crystal clear. Sometimes you have to search for them in places where only the heart can go."

"I still don't think I understand," I said.

"I hope you never do," my father said softly, "but from what the doctors at Broughton told me there's a chance you will."

My father leaned over, switched on the Buick's headlights.

"We need to get home," he said. "Your mother will be worried about us."

The pill bottles remained unopened the rest of the summer, and there were no more attempts to cauterize my father's despair with electricity. Which is not to say my father was a happy man. His was not a religion of bliss but one that allowed him to rise from his bed on each of those summer mornings and face two classes of hormone-ravaged adolescents, to lead those students toward solutions he himself no longer found adequate. I did not tell my mother what I had seen that Wednesday evening, or what I refused to see. I have never told her.

My father died that September, on an afternoon when the first reds and yellows flared in the maples and poplars. We'd driven up to the lake house that morning. My father graded tests until early afternoon. When he'd finished he went inside and put on his diving gear, then crossed the brief swath of grass to the water—moving slow and deliberate on the land like an aquatic creature returning to its natural element. Once on the dock he turned toward the lake house, raised a palm, and fell forever from us.

My mother and I sat on the porch playing Risk and drinking tea. When my father hadn't resurfaced after a reasonable time, my mother cast frequent glances toward the water.

"It hasn't been thirty minutes yet," I said more than once. But in a few more minutes half an hour had passed, and my father still had not risen.

I ran down to the lake while my mother dialed the county's

EMS unit. I dove into the murky water around the dock, finding nothing on the bottom but silt. I dove until the rescue squad arrived, though I dove without hope. I was seventeen years old. I didn't know what else to do.

The rest of the afternoon was a loud confusion of divers and boats, rescue squad members and gawkers. The sheriff showed up and, almost at dusk, the coroner, a young man dressed in khakis and a blue cotton shirt.

"Nitrogen narcosis, sometimes called rapture of the deep," the coroner said, conversant in the language of death despite his youth. "A lot of people wouldn't think a reservoir would be deep enough to cause that, but this one is." He and the sheriff stood with my mother and me on the screened porch, cups of coffee in their hands. "If you go down too far you can take in too much nitrogen. It causes a chemical imbalance, an intoxicating effect." The coroner looked out toward the reservoir. "It can happen to the most experienced diver."

The coroner talked to us a few more minutes before he and the sheriff stepped off the screened porch, leaving behind empty coffee cups, no doubt hoping what inevitable calamity would reunite them might wait until after a night's sleep.

ONCE HE HAD no further say in the matter, my father was again a Presbyterian. His funeral service was held at Cliffside Presbyterian, his burial in the church's cemetery. Mr. Holcombe and several of his congregation attended. They sat in the back, the men wearing short-sleeved shirts and ties, the women cotton dresses that reached their ankles. After the burial they awkwardly shook my hand and my mother's before departing. I've never seen any of them since.

In my less generous moments I perceive my mother's insistence on Presbyterian last rites as mean-spirited, a last rebuke to my father's Pentecostal reconversion. But who can really know another's heart? Perhaps it was merely her Scots-Irish practicality, less trouble for everyone to hold the rites in Cliffside instead of twenty miles away in the mountains.

After my father's death my mother refused to go back to the lake house, but I did and occasionally still do. I sit out on the screened porch as the night starts its slow glide across the lake. It's a quiet time, the skiers and most of the fishermen gone home, the echoing trombone of frogs not yet in full volume. I listen to sounds unheard any other time—the soft slap of water against the dock, a muskrat in the cattails.

I sometimes think of my father down in that murky water as his lungs surrendered. I think of what the coroner told me that night on the porch, that the divers found the mask in the silt beside him. "Probably didn't even know he was doing it," the coroner said matter-of-factly. "People do strange things like that all the time when they're dying."

The coroner is probably right. But sometimes as I sit on the porch with darkness settling around me, it is easy to imagine that my father pulling off the mask was something more—a gesture of astonishment at what he drifted toward.

❖

Last Rite

When the sheriff stepped onto her porch, he carried his hat in his hands, so she knew Elijah was dead. The sheriff told how drovers had found her son's body beside a spring just off the trail between Boone and Mountain City, a bullet hole in the back of his head, his pockets turned inside out. He told her of the charred piece of fatback in the skillet, the warm ashes underneath, the empty haversack with the name Elijah Hampton stitched into it. The drovers had nailed the skillet in a big beech tree as a marker and then buried him beside it.

"Murdered," Sarah said, speaking the word the sheriff had avoided. "For a few pieces of silver in his pocket."

It wasn't a question but the sheriff answered as if it were.

"That's what I reckon."

"And you don't know who done it."

"No, ma'am," the sheriff said. "And I'll not lie to you. We'll likely never know."

The sheriff held the haversack out to her.

"Your daughter-in law didn't want this. She said she couldn't bear the sight of his blood on it. You may not want it either."

Sarah took the haversack and laid it beside the door.

"So you've already been to see Laura," she said.

"Yes, ma'am. I thought it best, her being the wife."

The sheriff reached into his shirt pocket.

"Here's the death certificate. I thought you might want to see it."

"Just a minute," Sarah said. She stepped into the front room and took the Bible and pen from the mantel. She sat in her porch chair, the Bible open on her lap, the piece of paper in her hand.

"It don't say where he died," Sarah said.

"No, ma'am. That gap where they found him, it's the back of beyond. Nobody lives down there, ever has far as I know."

The sheriff looked down at her, his pale blue eyes shadowed by the hat he now wore.

"Mrs. Hampton," he said, "they don't even know what state that place is in, much less what county."

Sarah closed the Bible, the last line unfilled.

EIGHT MONTHS LATER the dew darkened the hem of her gingham dress as Sarah walked out of the yard, the cool slickness of the grass brushing her bare feet and ankles. She followed Aho

Creek down the mountain to where it entered the middle fork of the New River. She stepped onto the wagon road and followed the river north toward Boone, the sun rising over her right shoulder. Soon the river's white rush plunged away from the road. Her shoulder began aching, and she shifted the haversack to her other side.

Sarah stopped at a creek on the outskirts of town. She drank from the creek and unwrapped the sandwich she'd brought with her, but the first mouthful stuck in her throat like sawdust. She tore the bread and ham into pieces and left it for the birds before opening the haversack. Sarah knew she looked a sight but could do nothing about it except take out the lye soap and facecloth and wash the sweat from her face and neck, the dust from her feet and ankles. She took out her shoes and put them on and then walked into Boone, the main street crowded with farmers and their families come to spend Saturday in town. Sarah searched the storefronts until she found the sign that said BENEDICT ASH—SURVEYOR.

His age surprised her, the smooth brow, the full set of teeth. Like the unweathered sign outside his door, the youth made Sarah wonder how experienced he was. The surveyor must have realized clients would wish him older, for he wore a mangy red beard and a pair of wire-rimmed glasses he did not put on until Sarah appeared at his door. Sarah told him what she wanted and he listened, first with incredulity and then with resignation. He'd been in Boone less than a month and needed any client he could get.

When Sarah finished, the surveyor spread a map across his desk. He took off the glasses and studied the map intently before he spoke.

"My fee will be six dollars. It'll be a full day to get there, do the surveying, and get back. I don't work Sundays, so I'll go first thing Monday morning."

Sarah took a leather purse from the haversack, unsnapped it, and removed two silver dollars and four quarters.

"Here. I'll pay you the rest when you're done."

She poured the silver into his hand. "What time do we leave on Monday, Mr. Ash?"

"We?" he asked.

SUNDAY NIGHT SARAH had trouble falling asleep. She lay in bed thinking about how Laura had come to church that morning dressed in a blue cotton dress, her dark widow's weeds now packed away.

"You'd think she'd have worn them a year," Anna Miller whispered as they watched Laura enter the church with Clay Triplett.

"She has to get on with her life," Sarah replied without conviction. She watched Laura lean close to Clay Triplett as the singing began, their hands touching beneath the shared hymnal. Sarah tried to be charitable toward her daughter-in-law, reminding herself that Laura was barely nineteen, that she had been married to Elijah less than a year. The young could believe bad times would be balanced out by good. They could believe the past was something you could box up and forget.

After the service Sarah asked Laura if she wanted to make the journey with the surveyor and her. Sarah wasn't sure if it pleased or disappointed her when Laura said yes. Sarah asked to borrow one of the horses, offered to pay.

"You know I wouldn't charge you, Mrs. Hampton," Laura said. "I'll bring the horse over this afternoon on my way to Boone. I'll spend the night with my aunt in town."

Then Laura had walked over to where Clay Triplett waited in the shade of a live oak tree. He'd tipped his hat to Sarah, then helped Laura into his wagon to take her home.

It had been almost suppertime when Laura brought the horse.

"I reckoned you'd want Sapphire," Laura said. "Elijah always said she was your favorite."

Laura opened her grip and removed a photograph of Elijah taken when he was twelve years old. She handed the photograph to Sarah.

"I think it best if you keep this now. Something else to remember him by."

"Why are you giving me this?" Sarah asked.

Laura blushed. "Me and Clay, we're going to get married."

"I figured as much," Sarah said, her voice colder than she intended.

"I'd hoped you'd understand, Mrs. Hampton," Laura said.

Sarah looked at the photograph, Elijah dressed in his Sunday church clothes though it had been a Saturday morning in a photographer's studio in Boone. Elijah stared at her from a decade away, his eyes dark and serious.

"You keep it," Sarah finally said, handing the photograph back. "I won't forget what he looked like. You probably will."

Laura let the photograph lie on her open palms. She gazed intently, as though seeing something in it she had not noticed before.

"I loved Elijah," Laura said, not looking up.

"I still do," Sarah had replied.

Sapphire whinnied out in the barn, the same barn she had been foaled in seven springs ago. Will had died the previous winter, Sarah and Elijah had delivered the colt. Sarah wondered if Sapphire remembered the barn, remembered she had been born there.

In the darkness Sarah finally fell asleep and dreamed that Elijah was calling her. He was not the man he'd grown up to be. It was a child's voice Sarah heard in the laurel slick she stumbled and shoved through, branches welting her face and arms and legs as she thrashed deeper in the slick, her legs growing wearier with each blind step, the voice that called her never closer or farther away. Sarah woke with the quilt thrown off the bed, her brow damp as if fevered. She lay in the dark and waited for first light, remembering what was not dream but memory.

It had been August and Elijah was five. She and Will were hoeing the cornfield by the creek. She left Elijah at the end of a row, the whirligig Will had carved for him clasped in his hand. When she reached the end of the row, Elijah was gone. They searched all afternoon, working their way back to the farmhouse and then above the pasture where the woods thickened, the same woods where they had heard a panther that spring. She shouted his name until her throat was raw and her voice no more than a harsh whisper.

As night came on Will took the horse to get more help. Sarah lit the lantern and followed the creek, calling her son's name with what voice she had left. A half mile downstream he answered, his trembling voice rising out of a laurel slick that bordered the creek. She pushed and tripped through the laurel, making wrong guesses, losing her sense of direction in the tangle of leaves and branches. She found him lying on a matting of laurel leaves, the whirligig still clutched in his hand. That was just like him, Sarah thought. Even as a child he'd been careful not to lose things. Careful in other ways too, so that even at eight or nine he could be trusted with an ax or rifle.

SARAH AND LAURA met the surveyor Monday morning in front of his office. He had not bothered to wear the glasses, but an owls head pistol bulged from the holster on his hip.

"That three dollars," he said to Sarah. "I can take it now and lock it in my office."

"I'd just as lief wait till you earned it," Sarah replied.

They rode west out of Boone, she on Sapphire, Laura on the gray stallion Will had named Traveler, the surveyor on his roan. The land soon became steeper, rockier. Sarvis and beardtongue bloomed on the road's edge while dogwoods brightened the woods. The horses breathed harder as the air thinned. Sarah felt light-headed, but it was more than the altitude. She had been unable to eat any supper or breakfast.

They passed Oak Grove and Villas, then turned north, through Silverstone. Sarah wondered what people thought of this strange procession, of the armed young man wearing denim pants and a long-sleeved cotton shirt, the clanking surveying equipment draped on the roan's flanks like armor, the nineteen-year-old girl dressed in widow's weeds behind him, and Sarah last, also in black, holding the reins and a family Bible, forty-two but already an old woman. Sarah stared down at her hands and noted how coarse and wrinkled they were, how the purple veins stretched across their backs as if worms had burrowed under her skin.

Outside of Silverstone the wagon road narrowed until it was no longer a road but a trail. The Stone Mountains loomed like thunderheads. The surveyor carefully scanned the woods that pressed close to the trail and the stone outcrops they passed under, his free hand resting on his holster. Sarah felt Sapphire strain as the grade steepened and the thin air grew even thinner. A rattlesnake slithered across the path and she patted Sapphire's flank and spoke gently until the animal calmed. Sapphire remembered her, though the horse had been gone from the farm for nineteen months.

She had given Sapphire and the other two horses to Elijah the last morning he awoke under her roof. Sarah had fixed him breakfast but he was too excited to do anything except push the eggs and grits around his plate. Elijah talked of the house he was building at the foot of Dismal Mountain, the house where he and Laura would spend their first night together under an unshingled roof. Sarah called the horses a wedding gift though to her way of thinking they were already more his than hers. He had been the one who looked after them after Will died. Elijah had been only fourteen, but there had not been a morning or evening he forgot to feed or groom the horses. He'd treated the animals with care, like everything else in his life. Which was why he'd not ridden Sapphire to Mountain City. Elijah feared the mare might break a leg on the rocky backslope of the mountain. Always careful, Sarah thought, but somehow not careful enough with what was most precious of all.

They traveled another hour before entering the gap, the mountains and woods closing around them, sunlight mere glances in the treetops. No birds sang and no deer or rabbit bolted into the undergrowth at their approach. The trees leaned over the trail as if listening.

"I didn't know it to be this far," the surveyor grumbled. "To be honest, Mrs. Hampton, I don't believe six dollars is enough."

"My son lost his life for less money," Sarah said.

They came to the spring first, the bare, packed ground of a campsite beside it. They dismounted and let the horses drink. The skillet rusted on the big beech a few yards down the trail and in the woods behind it they found the swelling in the ground. Like it's pregnant, Sarah thought. The drovers had done as much as could be expected. A flat creek rock no bigger than her Bible leaned at the head of the grave. No markings were on it. A few broom sedge sprigs poked through the brown leaves that covered the grave. Another winter and Sarah knew the rock would fall, the grave settle, and no one would know a man was buried here.

She wondered if she'd be alive by then. Her stomach had troubled her for months. Ginseng and yellowroot, the draft the doctor had given her, did not help. She had no appetite, and last week she'd coughed up a bright gout of blood.

The surveyor spoke first. "I'm going to get my equipment and go a ways up that ridge." He pointed west, where a granite-faced mountain cut the sky in half. "It's too steep for the horses, so you all stay here. It shouldn't take me more than an hour," he said, then walked away.

Laura kneeled beside the grave and cleared the leaves from the mound. She took a handkerchief from her dress pocket and unknotted it.

"I brung some wildflower seeds to put on his grave," she said. "You want to help plant them, Mrs. Hampton?"

Sarah looked at Laura and realized why Elijah had been so smitten with her. The girl's eyes were dark as July blackberries, her hair yellow as corn silk. But pretty didn't last long in these mountains. Too soon, Sarah knew Laura would stand before a looking glass and find an old woman staring back.

"I'll help," Sarah said, and kneeled beside her daughter-in-law.

The ground was loose, so the planting didn't take very long. When they finished, Sarah stood, her hands stained by the dark loamy earth. "I'll be at the spring with the horses," she said.

She was tired from the journey, the night without sleep. She took the blanket off Sapphire and spread it on the ground where Elijah had died. She lay down and closed her eyes, the Bible laid beside her.

She slept and soon Elijah called her again. It was dark and she could see nothing, but he was close this time, just a few yards deeper into the laurel slick. Branches slashed at her face but she kept stumbling forward. She was close now, close enough to reach out her hand and touch his face.

"Mrs. Hampton."

The surveyor stood above her, the equipment burdening his shoulder, his face scratched and sweaty, one of his shirtsleeves torn.

"Where's Laura?" he asked.

"At the grave," Sarah said. Her right arm stretched out before her, open palm pressed to the rocky dirt. She raised that hand to shield her eyes, for it was now midday and sunlight fell through the trees straight as a waterfall.

"North Carolina, Watauga County," the surveyor said as he took a handkerchief from his pocket and wiped his brow. "Granite, yellow jackets, snakes, and briars, that's all that mountain is. I really think it only fair that you pay me two dollars extra. Why, just look at my shirt, Mrs. Hampton."

Sarah did not look up. She took the pen and bottle of ink from the haversack and opened the Bible. She found Elijah's name, his dates, and place of birth. Sarah clutched the pen and wrote each letter in slow, even strokes, her hand casting a shadow over the drying ink.

❖

Blackberries in June

On those August nights when no late-afternoon thunder-storm rinsed the heat and humidity from the air, no breeze stirred the cattails and willow oak leaves, Jamie and Matt sometimes made love surrounded by water. Tonight might be such a night, Jamie thought. She rolled down the window and let air blast away some of the cigarette smoke that clung to her uniform and hair. She was exhausted from eight hours of navigating tables with hardly a pause to stand still, much less sit down, from the effort it took to lift the sides of her mouth into an unwavering smile. Exhausted too from the work she'd done at the house before her shift at the restaurant. The radio in the decade-old Ford

Escort didn't work, so she hummed a Dixie Chicks song about chains being loosened. That's what she wanted, to be unchained in the weightlessness of water. She wanted to feel Matt lift and hold her so close their hearts were only inches apart.

In a few minutes the road fell sharply. At the bottom of the hill she turned off the blacktop onto what was, at least for now, more red-clay washout than road. The Escort bumped and jarred as it made its way down to the lake house. *Their* house, hers and Matt's. Barely a year married, hardly out of their teens, and they had a place they owned, not rented. It was a miracle Jamie still had trouble believing. And this night, like every night as she turned in to the drive, a part of her felt surprise the house was really there.

But it was, and already looking so much better than in June when she and Matt had signed the papers at the bank. What had been a tangle of kudzu and briars a yard and garden. Broken windows, rotted boards, and rust-rotten screens replaced. Now Jamie spent her mornings washing years of grime off walls and blinds. When that was done she could start caulking the cracks and gashes on the walls and ceilings. Matt reshingled the roof evenings after he got off, working until he could no longer see to nail. As he must have this night, because the ladder lay against the side of the house. In another month, when the shingles had been paid for, they would drive down to Seneca and buy paint. If things went well, in a year they'd have enough saved to replace the plumbing and wiring.

Matt waited on the screened-in porch. The light wasn't on but Jamie knew he was there. As she came up the steps his form emerged from the dark like something summoned out of air. He sat in the porch swing, stripped to his jeans. His work boots, shirt, and socks lay in a heap near the door. The swing creaked and swayed as she curled into his lap, her head against his chest. Her lips tasted the salty sweat on his skin as his arms pulled her closer. She felt the hardness of Matt's arms, muscled by two months of ten- to twelve-hour days cutting pulpwood. She wished of those hard muscles a kind of armor to protect him while he logged with her brother, Charlton, on the ridges where the Chauga River ran through Big Laurel Valley.

You best get a good look at your husband's pretty face right now, Charlton had said the first morning he came to pick up Matt. Feel the smooth of his skin too, little sister, because a man who cuts pulpwood don't stay pretty long.

Charlton had spoken in a joking manner, but she'd seen the certain truth of it in her brother's face, the broken nose and gapped smile, the raised, purple ridges on his arms and legs where flesh had been knitted back together. Jamie had watched Charlton as he and Matt walked to the log truck with its busted headlights and crumpled fender and cracked windshield. A truck no more beat-up and battered than its owner, Jamie had realized in that moment. Charlton was thirty years old, but he moved with the stiffness of an old man. Dr. Wesley in Seneca said he needed back surgery, but Charlton would hear nothing of it. Her sister-in-law, Linda, had told Jamie of nights Charlton drank half a bottle of whiskey to kill the pain. And sometimes, as Matt had witnessed, Charlton didn't wait until night.

The porch swing creaked as Jamie pressed her head closer to Matt's chest, close enough so she could not just hear but feel the strong, sure beat of his heart. First get the house fixed up, Jamie thought. Then when that was done she and Matt would start taking night classes again at the technical college. In a year they'd have their degrees. Then good jobs and children. It was a mantra she recited every night before falling asleep.

"Want to get in the lake?" Matt asked, softly kissing the top of her head.

"Yes," Jamie said, though she felt, to use her mother's words, tired to the bone. In some ways that was what made their love-making so good, especially on Saturday nights—finding in each other's bodies that last ounce of strength left from their long day, their long week, and sharing it.

They walked down the grassy slope to where a half-sunk pier leaned into the lake. On the bank they took off their clothes and stepped onto the pier, the boards trembling beneath them. At the pier's end the boards became slick with algae and water rose to their ankles. They felt for the drop-off with their feet, entered the water with a splash.

Then Jamie was weightless, the water up to her breasts, her feet lifting from the silt as she wrapped her arms around Matt. The sway of water eased away the weariness of eight hours of standing, eased as well the dim ache behind her eyes caused by hurry and noise and cigarette smoke. Water sloshed softly against the pier legs. The moon mirrored itself in the water, and Matt's head and shoulders shimmered in a yellow glow as Jamie raised her mouth to his.

THEY SLEPT LATE the next morning, then worked on the house two hours before driving up the mountain to her grandmother's for Sunday lunch. Behind the farmhouse a barn Jamie's grandfather had built in the 1950s crumbled into a rotting pile of tin and wood. In a white oak out by the boarded-up well, a cicada called for rain.

"Let's not stay more than an hour," Matt said as they stepped onto the front porch. "That's as long as I can stand Linda."

Inside, Jamie's parents, Charlton, Linda, and their children already sat at the table. Food was on the table and the drinks poured.

"About to start without you," Linda said sharply as they sat down. "When young ones get hungry they get contrary. If you had kids you'd know that."

"Them kids don't seem to be acting contrary to me," Matt said, nodding at the three children. "The only person acting contrary is their momma."

"I'm sorry," Jamie said. "We were working on the house and lost track of time."

"I know you all are trying to save money, but I still wish you had a phone," her mother said.

Grandma Chastain came in from the kitchen with a basket of rolls. She sat down at the table beside the youngest child.

"Say us a prayer, Luther," she said to her son.

For a few minutes they ate in silence. Then Charlton turned to his father.

"You ought to have seen the satinback me and Matt killed Wednesday morning. Eight rattles and long as my leg," Charlton said. "Them chain saws have made me so deaf I didn't even hear it. I'm just glad Matt did or I'd of sure stepped right on it."

"Don't tell such a thing, Charlton," Grandma Chastain said. "I worry enough about you out in them woods all day as it is."

"How's your back, Son?" Jamie's mother asked.

It was Linda who answered.

"Bothers him all the time. He turns all night in bed trying to get comfortable. Ain't neither of us had a good night's sleep in months."

"You don't think the surgery would do you good?" Grandma Chastain asked.

Charlton shook his head.

"It didn't help Bobby Hemphill's back none. Just cost him a bunch of money and a month not being able to work."

When they'd finished dessert, Jamie's mother turned to her.

"You want to go with me and Linda to that flower show in Seneca?"

"I better not," Jamie said. "I need to work on the house."

"You and Matt are going to work yourselves clear to the bone fixing that house if you're not careful," her mother said.

Jamie's father winked at Jamie.

"Your momma's always looking for the dark cloud in a blue sky."

"I do no such thing, Luther Alexander," her mother said. "It's just the most wonderful kind of thing that Jamie and Matt have that place young as they are. It's like getting blackberries in June. I just don't want them wearing themselves out."

"They're young and healthy, Momma. They can handle it," Charlton said. "Just be happy for them."

Linda sighed loudly and Charlton's lips tightened. The smile vanished from his face. He stared at his wife but did not speak. Instead, it was Grandma Chastain who spoke.

"You two need to be in church on Sunday morning," she said to Jamie, "not working on that house. You've been blessed, and you best let the Lord know you appreciate it."

"Look at you," Linda said angrily to Christy, the youngest child. "You got that pudding all over your Sunday dress." She yanked the child from her chair. "Come on, we're going to the bathroom and clean that stain, for what little good it'll do."

Linda walked a few steps, then turned back to the table, her hand gripping Christy's arm so hard the child whimpered.

"I reckon we all don't get lucky with lake houses and such," Linda said, looking not at Matt but at Jamie, "but that don't mean we don't deserve just as much. You just make sure your husband saves enough of his strength to do the job Charlton's overpaying him to do."

"I reckon if Charlton's got any complaints about me earning my pay he can tell me his own self," Matt said.

Linda swatted Christy's backside with her free hand.

"You hush now," she said to the child and dragged her into the bathroom.

For a few moments the only sound was the ticking of the mantel clock.

"You don't pay Linda no mind," Charlton said to Matt. "The smartest thing I done in a long while is let go that no-account Talley boy and hire you. You never slack up and you don't call in sick on Mondays. You ain't got a dime from me you ain't earned."

"And I wouldn't expect otherwise," Matt said.

"Still, it's a good thing Charlton's done," Jamie's mother said as she got up, "especially letting you work percentage." She laid her hand on her son's shoulder as she reached around him to pick up his plate. "You've always been good to look after your sister, and I know she'll always be grateful, won't you, girl?"

"Yes, ma'am," Jamie said.

The bathroom door opened and Christy came out trailing her mother, her eyes swollen from crying.

"We ought to be going," Matt said, pushing back his chair. "I need to get some more shingles on that roof."

"You shouldn't to be in such a rush," Grandma Chastain said, but Matt was already walking toward the door.

Jamie pushed back her chair.

"We do need to be going."

"At least let me wrap you up something for supper," Grandma Chastain said.

Jamie thought about how much work they had to do and how good it would be not to have to cook.

"Okay, Grandma," she said.

MATT WAS IN the car when she came out, the engine running and his hands gripping the steering wheel. Jamie placed the leftovers in the backseat and got in beside Matt.

"You could have waited for me," she said.

"If I'd stayed any longer I'd of said some things you wouldn't want me to," Matt said, "and not just to Linda. Your mother and grandma need to keep their advice to themselves."

"They just care about me," Jamie said, "about us."

They drove back to the house in silence and worked until dusk. As Jamie cleaned the blinds she heard Matt's hammer tapping above as if he was nailing her shut inside the house. She thought about the rattlesnake, how it could easily have bitten Matt, and remembered twelve years earlier, when her mother and Mr. Jenkins, the elementary school principal, appeared at the classroom door.

"Your daddy's been hurt," her mother said. Charlton was outside waiting in the logging truck, and they drove the fifteen miles to the county hospital. Her father had been driving a skid loader that morning. It had rained the night before and the machine had turned over on a ridge. His hand was shattered in two places, and there was nerve damage as well. Jamie remembered stepping into the white room with her mother and seeing her father in the bed, a morphine drip jabbed into his arm like a fang. If that skidder had turned over one more time you'd be looking at a dead man, her father had told them. Charlton had quit high school and worked full-time cutting pulpwood to make sure food was on the table that winter. Her father eventually got a job as a night watchman, a job, unlike cutting pulpwood, a man needed only one good hand to do.

"I GET SCARED for you, for us," Jamie said that night as they lay in bed. "Sometimes I wish we'd never had the chance to buy this place."

"You don't mean that," Matt said. "This place is the best thing that might ever happen to us. How many chances do young folks get to own a house on a lake? If we hadn't seen Old Man Watson's sign before the real-estate agents did, they'd have razed the house and sold the lot alone to some Floridian at twice what we paid."

"I know that," Jamie said, "but I can't help being scared for you. It's just like things have been too easy for us. Look at Charlton. Him and Linda have been married ten years and they're still in a trailer. Linda says good luck follows us around like a dog that needs petting all the time. She thinks you and me getting this house is just one more piece of luck."

"Well, the next time she says that you tell her anybody with no better sense than to have three kids the first five years she's married can't expect to have much money left for a down payment on a house, especially with a skidder to pay off as well."

Matt turned his head toward her. She could feel the stir of his breath.

"Linda's just jealous," he said, "that and she's still pissed off Charlton's paying me percentage. Linda best be worrying about her own self. She's got troubles enough at home without stirring up troubles for other people."

"You mean Charlton's drinking?"

"Yeah. Every morning this week he's reeked of alcohol, and it ain't his aftershave. The money they waste on whiskey and her on makeup and fancy hairdos could help make a down payment, not to mention that Bronco when they already had a perfectly good car. Damn, Jamie, they got three vehicles and only two people to drive them."

Matt placed his hand on the back of Jamie's head, letting his fingers run through her cropped hair, hair shorter than his. His voice softened.

"You make your own luck," Matt said. "Some will say we're lucky when you're working in a dentist's office and I'm a shift supervisor in a plant, like we hadn't been planning that very life since we were juniors in high school. They'll forget they stayed at home nights and watched TV instead of taking classes at Tech. They'll forget how we worked near full-time jobs in high school and saved that money when they wasted theirs on new trucks and fancy clothes."

"I know that," Jamie said. "But I get so tired of people acting resentful because we're doing well. It even happens at the café. Why can't they all be like Charlton, just happy for us?"

"Because it reminds them they're too lazy and undisciplined to do it themselves," Matt said. "People like that will pull you down with them if you give them the chance, but we're not going to let them do that to us."

Matt moved his hand slowly down her spine, letting it rest in the small of the back.

"It's time to sleep, baby," he said.

Soon Matt's breathing became slow and regular. He shifted in the bed and his hand slipped free from her back. First, get the house fixed up, she told herself as she let her weariness and the sound of tree frogs and crickets carry her toward sleep.

TWO MORE WEEKS passed, and it was almost time for Jamie to turn the calendar nailed by the kitchen door. She knew soon the leaves would start to turn. Frost would whiten the grass and she and Matt would sleep under piles of quilts Grandma Alexander had sewn. They'd sleep under a roof that no longer leaked. After Charlton picked up Matt, Jamie caulked the back room, the room that would someday be a nursery. As she filled in cracks she envisioned the lake house when it was completely renovated—the walls bright with fresh paint, all the leaks plugged, a porcelain tub and toilet, master bedroom built onto the back. Jamie imagined summer nights when children slept as she and Matt walked hand in hand down to the pier, undressing each other to share again the unburdening of water.

Everything but the back room's ceiling had been caulked

when she stopped at one-thirty to eat lunch and change into her waitress's uniform. She was closing the front door when she heard a vehicle bumping down through the woods to the house. In a few moments she saw her father's truck, behind the windshield his distraught face. At that moment something gave inside her, as if her bones had succumbed to the weight of the flesh they carried. The sky and woods and lake seemed suddenly farther away, as if a space had been cleared that held only her. She closed her hand around the key in her palm and held it so tight her knuckles whitened. Her father kicked the cab door open with his boot.

"It's bad," he said, "real bad." He didn't cut off the engine or get out from behind the wheel. "Linda and Matt and your momma are already at the hospital."

She didn't understand, not at first. She tried to picture a situation where her mother and Linda and Matt could have been hurt together—a car wreck, or fire—something she could frame and make sense of.

"Momma and Linda are hurt too?" Jamie finally asked.

"No," her father said, "just Charlton." His voice cracked. "They're going to have to take your brother's leg off, baby."

Jamie understood then, and at that moment she felt many things, including relief that it wasn't Matt.

WHEN THEY ENTERED the waiting room, her mother and Linda sat on a long green couch. Matt sat opposite them in a blue plastic chair. Dried blood stained his work shirt and jeans. He stood up, his face pale and haggard as he embraced her. Jamie smelled the blood as she rested her head against his chest.

"We were cleaning limbs," Matt said, "and the saw jumped back and dug into his leg till it got to bone. I made a tourniquet with my belt, but he still like to have bled to death." Matt paused. "Charlton shouldn't have been running that saw. He'd been drinking."

Matt held her close a few more moments, then stepped back. He nodded toward the corner where Linda and her mother sat.

"You better say something to your momma and Linda," he said and released her arms. Jamie let go too. It was only then that she realized the key was still in her closed right hand. She slipped it into her uniform pocket.

Her mother stood when Jamie approached, but Linda stayed on the couch, her head bowed.

"Pray hard, girl," her mother said as she embraced Jamie. "Your brother is going to need every prayer he can get."

"You seen him yet, Momma?" she asked. Jamie smelled the Camay soap her mother used every night. She breathed deep, let the smell of the soap replace the smell of blood.

"No, he's still in surgery, will be for at least another hour."

Her mother released her and stepped back.

"I can't stand myself just sitting here," she said and nodded at Jamie's father standing beside the door marked SURGERY. "Come on, Luther. I'm going to get us all some doughnuts and coffee and I need you to help carry it." She turned to Jamie. "You stay here and look after Linda."

Jamie sat in the place her mother had left. Linda's head re-mained bowed, but her eyes were open. Jamie looked up at the wall clock. Two-twenty-three. The red minute hand went around seven more times before Jamie spoke.

"It's going to be all right, Linda," she said. It was the only thing she could think to say.

Linda lifted her head, looked right at Jamie. "You sound pretty sure of that. Maybe if it was your husband getting his leg took off you'd think different."

Linda wasn't thirty yet, but Jamie saw something she recognized in every older woman in her family. It was how they looked out at the world, their eyes resigned to bad times and trouble. I don't ever remember being young, Grandma Alexander had once told her. All I remember is something always needing to be done, whether it was hoeing a field or the washing or feeding hungry children or cows or chickens.

The elevator door opened and Jamie's parents stepped out, their hands filled with paper bags.

"You think this couldn't have happened to Matt," Linda said, raising her voice enough that Jamie's parents came no closer. "You think it happened because Charlton had been drinking."

"I don't think any such thing," Jamie said.

Linda looked at her in-laws.

"I got three young ones to feed and buy school clothes for, and a disability check ain't going to be enough to do that."

"We'll do everything we can to help you," Jamie's father said and offered Linda a cup of coffee. "Here. This will give you some strength."

"I don't need strength," Linda said, her voice wild and angry. "I need the money Charlton overpaid Matt. Money that should be ours. Money we need worse than they do."

Linda looked at her father-in-law.

"You know Charlton paid hourly wages to everybody else who worked for him."

"I earned every cent he paid me," Matt said. He had left his seat and stepped closer, standing next to Jamie now. "I been there every day and I've cut plenty of days dawn to dark. It's bad what's happened to Charlton, and I'm sorry it happened. But me and Jamie don't owe you anything." Jamie placed her hand on Matt's arm, but he jerked it away. "I ain't listening to this anymore."

"You owe us everything," Linda shouted as Matt walked toward the elevator. "If Charlton hadn't taken you on you'd never have been able to make a down payment on that lake house." Linda looked at Jamie's parents now, tears streaming down her face. "A lake house, and the five of us in a beat-up double-wide."

The surgery room door opened, and a nurse glared at them all briefly before the door closed again.

Jamie's mother sat down on the couch and pressed Linda's head to her bosom. "We're all going to do everything possible to get you all through this, and that includes Matt and Jamie," she said.

Linda sobbed now, her face smeared with mascara. Minutes passed before she raised her head. She tried to smile as she brushed tears from her cheeks and slowly lifted herself from the couch. Jamie's father gripped Linda's upper arm when her knees buckled.

"I know I look a sight," Linda said. "I best go to the bathroom and tidy up so Charlton won't see me like this." She looked at Jamie. "I'm sorry," she said.

Jamie's father walked Linda to the restroom and waited by the door.

"Come here, girl," her mother said to Jamie.

Jamie didn't move. She was afraid, almost as afraid as when she'd seen her father's face through the windshield.

"I need to call the restaurant, let them know what's going on."

"That can wait a few minutes," her mother said. "We need to talk, and right now."

Jamie remained where she was.

"I know you're put out with Linda," her mother said, "and I don't blame you. Grieving don't give her no excuse to talk that way to you and Matt." She paused, waited for Jamie to meet her eyes. "But you know you got to help them."

Jamie turned and stared at the wall clock. She thought how only two hours earlier she had been caulking the back room of the lake house.

"Me and your daddy will do what we can, but that won't be near enough. Your daddy says even if the skidder's sold, it'll bring no more than two thousand dollars. We're not talking about just Linda here. We're talking about your niece and nephews."

"Why are you saying this to me, Momma?" Jamie asked. "Matt's going to have to find another job now, and there's no way he'll make the kind of money Charlton paid him. We need all the money we got just to make the payments on the lake house, much less fix it up. We'll have tuition to pay as well come spring."

The elevator door opened. Jamie hoped it was Matt, but a chaplain got off and walked past them toward the intensive care unit.

"You've been blessed, Jamie," her mother said. "Linda's right. Charlton never let anyone but Matt work percentage. You could give Charlton the difference between what Matt got paid and the six dollars an hour anybody else would have got."

"But we'd have to sell the lake house," Jamie said. "How can you ask me and Matt to do that?"

"The same way I'd have asked your brother to quit high school. Only I never had to ask. He knew what had to be done and did it without me saying a word to him. Seventeen years old and he knew what had to be done." Her mother laid her hand on Jamie's. "That lake house, you had no right to expect such a place so young. You know it was a miracle you got it in the first place. You can't expect miracles in this life, girl."

The bathroom door opened and Linda came out. She and Jamie's father walked toward them.

"Maybe not, Momma," Jamie said, her voice low but sharp, "but when they come a person's got a right to take them."

"You got to do what's best for the whole family," her mother said, speaking quietly as well. "You got to accept that life is full of disappointments. That's something you learn as you grow older."

THERE HAD BEEN complications during the surgery, and Jamie was unable to see Charlton until after seven-thirty. His eyes opened when she placed her hand on his, but he was too drugged to say anything coherent. Jamie wondered if he even understood what had happened to him. She hoped that for a little while longer he didn't.

When Jamie and Matt got back to the lake house it was dark, and by then things had been decided, but not before harsh words had been exchanged.

"Come on," Matt said, reaching for her hand after they got out of the Escort. "Let's go down to the lake, baby. I need one good thing to happen in my life today."

"Not tonight," Jamie said. "I'm going on in."

She changed into her nightgown. Matt came in soon afterward naked and dripping, work clothes and boots cradled in his arms. Jamie stepped out of the bathroom, a toothbrush in her hand.

"Put those clothes out on the porch," she said. "I don't want to smell that blood anymore."

Jamie was in bed when he came back, and soon Matt cut out the light and joined her. For a minute the only sounds were the crickets and tree frogs. The mattress's worn-out springs creaked as Matt turned to face her.

"I'll go see Harold Wilkinson in the morning," he said. "He knows I did good work for Charlton. I figure I can get eight dollars an hour to work on his crew, especially since I know how to run a skidder."

He reached out and laid his arm on Jamie's shoulder.

"Come here," he said, pulling her closer.

She smelled the thick, fishy odor of the lake, felt the lake's coldness on his skin.

"They'll be needing help a long time," Matt said. "In two, three years at most we'll have jobs that pay three times what we're making now. Keeping this house is going to save us a lot of money, money we can help them with later."

Matt paused.

"You listening to me?"

"Yes," Jamie said.

"Linda's parents can help too. I didn't hear your momma say a word about them helping out." Matt kissed her softly on the cheek. "They'll be all right. We'll all be all right. Go to sleep, babe. You got another long day coming."

But she did not fall asleep, not for a while, and she woke at first light. She left the bed and went to the bathroom. Jamie turned on the faucet and soaked a washcloth, wrung it out and pressed it to her face. She set it on the basin and looked at the mirror. A crack jagged across the glass like a lightning bolt, a crack caulk couldn't fill. Something else to be replaced.

❖

Not Waving but Drowning

Across the room a woman holds her front teeth in the palm of her hand. She stares at them as if they were a bad throw of the dice. The man who brought her through the emergency room door leans his cheek against her swollen face. "You know I love you," he whispers. Her hand tightens around the teeth. A red drool is all she can get out before clamping her mouth shut, leaning her head back against the wall. The man yanks a soiled handkerchief from his back pocket. He wets the cloth with his spit and wipes blood from her mouth and chin.

I turn to see if Mary is watching, but her eyes are closed, her lips moving. For a moment I think she is praying, but she is doing what we learned at our Lamaze classes, counting to ten, then exhaling, slow and steady. Her hand presses her belly, as if the spread fingers might somehow hold inside what's been there four months. I place my hand over hers, wanting to believe the weight of another hand might make a difference to the baby, to Mary. She takes away my hand, and I remember what she said as we sped here, the road coiling around the black silence of Lake Jocassee where this night began one afternoon four months ago.

"It's our baby, not just yours," I'd said when she wouldn't answer my questions.

"Not yet," Mary had said. "Not until it's born. Only then is it ours."

A big man dressed in jeans and a black, long-sleeved dress shirt shoulders through the door. His right hand is swollen like a snakebite, the knuckles scraped raw. The receptionist, a gray-haired woman in a white nursing uniform, has disappeared. When she comes back she shoves a clipboard through a hole in the bottom of the glass that separates her from the circle of metal folding-back chairs filled with varying degrees of misfortune. The man clutches the wrist below the damaged hand and raises it.

"Can't, ma'am. It's broken."

The gray-haired woman pulls the clipboard back to her side, places her pencil on the first line.

"Name," she says, not even looking at him.

I don't hear his name. I'm thinking eleven months back to another night, July, not June, but a night like this, muggy, loud with tree frogs and crickets. I'm thinking about how I'd woke in the dark and Mary was crying. A nightmare, I thought, and pulled her to me and felt what was too sticky to be sweat staining her skin. I touched a damp finger to my tongue and tasted blood.

"What's happened?" I asked.

"The baby," she said.

So we dressed and came here and sat in maybe these same two chairs and waited to be told what we already knew. The doctor said Mary should stay overnight and they gave her a blue pill, and when the pill had done its work I drove home and pulled the sheets off the bed only to find the blood had soaked onto the mattress pad. So I pulled it off too and saw on the mattress a black spot like a water stain. Maybe it was lack of sleep, but for a moment I was convinced it had gone through the mattress and would cover the whole room if I didn't contain it. I jerked the mattress off. Through the box springs I saw there was no blood on the floor.

I bundled up the sheets and mattress pad and carried them into the backyard. I dragged the mattress out there too, then soaked everything with lighter fluid and listened to the crackle of the fire, the tree frogs and crickets and a far-off owl. I was back at the hospital by first light.

Mary didn't speak on the drive home. I let her wrap herself in silence. I pulled around to the back so she wouldn't have but a few steps. She saw the charred mattress, the wisps of smoke that rose toward a sky that promised a day without rain.

"You think it's that simple," she said.

The man with the broken hand sits down next to the entrance. I look at my watch—seventeen minutes since we came in. I step up to the window, bend to speak through the hole in the glass, but the woman is gone. The door at the back of her office is half open. I see that it leads to the other emergency room, the one where they carry you in on a stretcher. The receptionist finally comes back, leaves the door cracked behind her.

"We have to see the doctor now," I tell her. "My wife may be having a miscarriage. Please," I say.

"Just a few minutes more and the doctor will be free," she says. "There's two boys next door." The woman nods toward the room she has just come from. "They've been in a car wreck. Those boys are in bad shape."

"My wife's in bad shape too," I say. "The baby is."

"I understand," she says.

I sit back down.

"Just a few more minutes," I tell Mary. "It won't be long."

Mary looks at me but says nothing.

"She's a cold bitch, ain't she?" the man next to the door says to me.

"What?" I say, hoping I heard wrong, because if I didn't I know this conversation will end with an exchange of fists.

He nods toward the receptionist's glassed-in cubicle.

"I say she's a cold one."

I look up to see if the receptionist has heard, but she's gone. The phone rings.

"They give them enough breaks," the man next to the door says. "Damn if I don't think I'll put me in a application here. Where I work they won't let you go to the bathroom but once a shift."

"Where you work?" asks the man with the woman holding the teeth.

"Hamrick Mill."

The man nods at the woman beside him.

"Her brother worked there a few months. He said they'd treat you like a dog if you'd let them. He wouldn't put up with that so they fired him."

"What's his name?"

"Billy Goins."

"Don't remember him."

"Like I said, he wasn't there but a couple of months."

The woman stares at the teeth in her hand.

"Is that your wife?"

"Yes."

The woman doesn't look up. It's as if she's deaf. Maybe she is. Maybe she's like the Cambodian women I've read about, the ones who witnessed so many atrocities that they have willed themselves blind. Maybe that's what you have to do sometimes to survive. You kill off a part of yourself, your hearing or eyesight, your capacity for hope.

"What happened to her?" The moment he speaks the man with the hurt hand seems to realize the answer. "I mean she's going to be okay, isn't she?"

"Accident," the husband answers. He places his arm around his wife's hunched shoulders. "She's going to be fine."

The door that leads into the examining rooms opens halfway. An intern, probably not even thirty, grips the door's edge with both hands and leans his head in as if afraid to come among us. He glances at the couple across the room and then at Mary and me.

"Mrs. Triplett?" he asks, looking at Mary.

Mary keeps her hand on her belly as I ease her to her feet. I walk her to where the doctor holds the door open.

"You stay here," she says. "I don't want you with me. Not until I know."

I start to speak.

"No," Mary says, her voice rising. "You stay here."

So I do. The others have been listening. When I sit back down, the man by the door picks up a tattered *Sports Afield* with his good hand and stares at the cover. The man with the woman takes a jackknife from his pocket and pares his nails. His wife is the only one who looks at me.

I lean my head back against the wall and close my eyes, think about the day four months back that brought Mary and me to this place, one of those late February days you get around here, a kind of miracle when the sky opens up deep and blue and the temperature rises into the seventies. It's more than weather a couple of weeks ahead of schedule. There's no wind like there is in March or early April. It's like you've leapfrogged two months. All that's missing are the dogwood blossoms.

Mary said we should fix a picnic lunch and go to Lake Jocassee, take the boat out and eat our lunch on the far shore, where the Horsepasture River enters the lake. I was glad she wanted to leave the house, gladder still she wanted to do something with me. Since the second miscarriage she hadn't wanted to do much of anything but sit at home on weekends and stare at the television. We'd been more like roommates than husband and wife.

I hadn't taken the boat out since September, so I checked it good before I hitched the boat trailer onto the car. Mary stayed inside and made our lunch.

We were on the water by ten. Since there was no wind, I cut the motor halfway across and we drifted. We looked down into mountain water so clear it was like peering through a window. After a few minutes we saw what we were looking for. Eighty feet down were farmhouses Duke Power hadn't bothered to raze when they'd built the dam, and not just houses but barns, woodsheds, even mailboxes. Everything was there but the people.

"It's like if you watched long enough somebody would walk out of one of those houses and look up and wave at us the same way we'd look up and wave at a plane," Mary said, and her saying that spooked me, because I'd been thinking the same thing, not the part about the plane but that there were still people down there, people who didn't know they were buried under eighty feet of water.

I'd moored the boat in the cove where the Horsepasture slowed and lost itself in the lake. We walked a quarter mile through woods that still had patches of snow and spread a quilt in a meadow we'd found years back right after we'd gotten married. It had been cool on the water and in the woods, but here the noon sun poured down on us. The surrounding oaks and poplars seemed to wedge all the sun's heat into the meadow. A few wildflowers opened their petals. I took off my sweatshirt.

Mary unpacked cheese, apples, a loaf of bread, and a bottle of wine from the picnic basket. I'd been expecting turkey sandwiches and Cokes. Neither one of us had ever been much of a wine drinker, and I almost said something about that but I didn't. Mary seemed happy, and she hadn't been happy for a long time.

"Here," she said, handing me the wine, paper cups, and corkscrew, "make yourself useful."

In the distance I could hear the last waterfall before the river entered the lake, but I heard nothing else. No boat motors, no squirrels or birds. You could almost have believed there was no world beyond the meadow's tree line. I handed Mary a cup of wine.

"To the future," she said and tapped her cup against mine. She took a sip, then placed the cup on the grass and did not drink from it again.

Our appetites were keen. We ate all the bread and cheese and halved an apple. When we finished we put everything back in the basket and lay down on the quilt, drowsy from the food and warmth. I was almost asleep when Mary sat up and unlaced her hiking boots. She took off her sweatshirt. There was nothing, not even a bra, underneath. Mary lay down beside me and took off her jeans and then unbuttoned my shirt. I was surprised because I knew that it was the time of month she was most fertile. Since the second miscarriage she hadn't let me touch her during this time, even with her diaphragm in. I felt the goose bumps on her arms, so I folded the quilt over us.

"What about your diaphragm?" I asked.

"I want us to try again," she said and pulled me to her.

We slept afterward. I woke before Mary and listened to her breath merge with the sound of the waterfall. I lay there knowing our future together would come down to this last gamble, because our marriage had barely survived the last miscarriage. If it had survived. I wasn't sure.

Something happens to a couple after a miscarriage, or at least it had happened to us. You cry together, you talk to the counselor and preacher, you hear the same stupid and callous remarks from friends and kin who should know better, but there's still a part of the pain you can't share, even with the person who went through it with you. You carry that pain inside like a tumor, and though it may shrink with time, it never disappears, and it's malignant.

Shadows had covered us by the time Mary waked. She'd pressed against me and we'd made love again, then walked back into the woods, leaving behind the last rays of sunshine filtering through the trees, the wildflowers that would die in a few days, when the frost returned.

I open my eyes, try to believe Mary's going to come through the door, smile, and say everything is okay. The woman across the room is still looking at me. She opens her mouth, slow like a rusty hinge. Her forehead creases. She speaks, a mumble of blood and words that I can't understand.

"No, darling," her husband says, placing his arm around her. "Don't try to talk."

Up the highway toward Westminster I hear an ambulance, the wail increasing as it nears, then silenced as it turns in to the emergency entrance, red light drenching all of us as it passes the glass door Mary and I hurried through an hour ago.

The phone at the reception desk rings.

"Mr. Triplett." The receptionist motions for me.

I walk over to the window.

"Dr. Walton needs to talk with you. He's down the corridor, second room on the right."

Her voice is muffled by the glass. She points at the door as if we are in a place where we can communicate only in gestures.

I look back at the woman with the battered face. Her brown eyes hold mine for a moment. She nods, and I want to believe that both our lives might somehow turn out better than either of us can believe at this moment. Not tomorrow or next week, just sometime. I take a deep breath and walk through the door that says DO NOT ENTER and down the corridor. I walk slow as the dead might walk across the cold and silent floor of Lake Jocassee.

Overtime

Luther comes up to me right before quitting time. He wants to go over to Holly Oak Park in Shelby and play some ball. I'm thinking how dog tired I am now and how much tireder I'll be tomorrow if I play. But it is Thursday. You can always get through Friday, no matter how tired, sick, or hungover you are. It's like getting to the fourth quarter and knowing you just got to gut it out a little longer.

"What time you want me to pick you up?" I ask. His old lady works the suicide shift at the 7-Eleven, so she'll have the car.

"Seven," he says. "I'll get us a six-pack for after."

"You don't have to do that," I say, but I know he does. He's too proud to just bum a ride, especially from a white guy.

We walk to the trailer to clock out, moving slow to make sure it's not a second before five o'clock when we get there. Luther gets his card and punches it. His hands and arms are no more black than mine are white. Since we mix mortar all day, we're mostly gray from the shirtsleeves down, like a new race of people.

Luther walks on out to where the hourly workers park, and I follow him. Even from the back you can tell he's still in shape. No spare tire. Still wiry strong. When he played safety in high school, he was only five-eight and 135 pounds, but man could he hit. In the Burns game my senior year, their fullback ran right by me and everybody else on the line. Our linebackers were blitzing, so it was just Luther and this two-hundred-pound fullback who wasn't even going to try to run around Luther, just plow right through him. They had to carry that son of a bitch off the field on a stretcher. Luther cracked three of his ribs. That guy spent the rest of the game on the bench, moaning and spitting up blood.

I GET TO Luther's place right at seven. It's not much, a double-wide, a few scraggly-assed pine trees, and a lot of red dirt for a front yard. But unlike me he at least owns his place. That's something. An old woman peeks through the curtains. Luther's five-year-old comes out, runs up to my window.

"Daddy say he'll be out in a minute," she says. Then she runs like hell back to the trailer, maybe to finish her dessert or watch a cartoon. I sit and think how we haven't done too bad, me and Luther. At least we aren't inside Calhoun Mills sucking up cotton dust all day and coughing it back up all night, like our daddies did. And unlike most of the guys we played football with in high school, our knees aren't zippered and our backs aren't hurting all the time.

Luther finally comes out. He's got a six-pack of Miller in one hand and shoes and socks in the other.

"Sorry," he says. "Got stuck at the bank after work. You ever seen one of them loan applications?"

I tell him I have, but it's clear he doesn't want to talk about it, probably didn't even mean to bring it up. He looks out the window and I concentrate on navigating the washed-out piece of shit the county calls a road.

When we walk into the gym, nobody else white is around. Which isn't any big surprise, Holly Oak being on the black side of Shelby. But I work with a couple of the guys, played football with a couple more, and I'm with Luther, so everything is cool. They're playing half-court, which is fine by me. I smoke too much to have any wind. Two guys in the bleachers say they've got the next game, but they take us and one guy off the losing team. I walk over to a side basket to stretch a little and shoot a few baskets, but I've barely got my sweats off when it's our game.

Winners get the ball, so their point guard, a guy I don't know, dribbles out to half-court. Luther guards him. This guy takes about two dribbles before Luther picks his pocket, wings me a pass, and I lay it in. After that I set a few picks and pull down a few boards, but it's Luther's show. He's pushing thirty-two, but he's still quick as lightning and slick as owl shit. As good as Luther was in football in high school, he was even better in basketball. A lot of people thought he was second best on the team our senior year. Luther played basketball like he played football, all out and physical, elbows and knees like raw hamburger from diving after loose balls.

We're up 13–3 when Cedric comes in. Their big guy has the ball and I'm guarding him close, but he just stops dribbling, stares over at the door like he's just seen a ghost.

I don't recognize Cedric at first. He's skinny, skinnier than in high school. Cocaine can do that to you. He's got on an NBA sweat suit, the kind you can't buy at a sporting goods store or even order from a catalog.

He's carrying a gym bag in his right hand. Then someone says, "Cedric," and I know for sure.

"Let's play," says Luther, snatching the ball from their center's hands, throwing it to their point guard a little too hard. "Take it out."

They do and I get a rebound, Luther hits a jump shot, and a drive, and the game's over. The losers walk over to Cedric, and a couple of the guys on our team join them. I walk over to the water fountain. Luther's out at midcourt. He bounces the ball hard against the floor.

"Let's play," Luther yells, but nobody's listening.

I get my water, try to decide if I want to go over and say hello to Cedric. We'd known each other since first grade, played football together in junior high and been in the same classes until our junior year, when it became clear he'd be getting scholarship offers. After that they'd put him in college prep. We'd still seen each other some, mainly in the weight room. But that was half a life ago. I didn't want to risk going up to him, having to explain who I was and then him having to pretend he remembered. I walked over anyway, but let him speak first.

"Ricky, my main man," he says, raising his hand for a high five. "How's it going?"

There's not many people I look up to, but Cedric is six-six. I have to stretch to slap palms.

"What's with the beard?" He reaches out and gives it a tug. "You trying to look like that Manson dude?" He pushes my hair back. "Gotta check and make sure you haven't got an *x* carved in your forehead."

It feels good, his kidding, his remembering me. "How you doing, Cedric?" I ask.

"Great, man," he says. "I was telling these guys Boston wants me to fly up for a tryout. Told them I had to come home and see my momma first. Told them I need some home cooking to sustain me."

Everybody laughs. We hope it's true, but I'm close enough to smell liquor on his breath. His eyes are bloodshot.

"Let's play," yells Luther. He's still at midcourt, but he takes a few steps toward us. "This your game, Jo-Jo?" he asks. Jo-Jo played football with us back in high school. He nods.

"Well, get your black ass and whoever you got playing with you out here," Luther says.

Jo-Jo turns to Cedric. "You want to play with us?"

"Sure," Cedric says. "Just give me a minute to put on my brace."

I go out to midcourt with our other guys. Charles, who plays forward, turns to Luther.

"Who's gonna try to guard him?" Charles asks.

I'm the tallest, the only one who is even close to Cedric's height, but even with Cedric wearing the knee brace, there's no way in hell I'm quick enough. He'd have to be in a damn wheelchair for me to stay with him. Charles is six feet, and he's fairly quick, world-class speed compared to me.

"I'll take him," says Luther.

It takes five minutes for Cedric to get the brace on. There are all sorts of snaps and locks. Everybody, even Luther, is watching him put it on, all of us knowing how he'd hurt his knee, not on the court but outside a bar in Detroit.

Luther takes the ball out, passes to Charles, who's being guarded by Cedric. Charles fakes left, dribbles right, and goes by Cedric for a layup, and it's clear nobody has called or is going to call from Boston or anywhere else. Luther takes the ball out, passes it to Charles again. Charles must be wanting another story to tell his grandkids because he fakes left again. But this time Cedric just backs up, cuts off the lane to the basket. Charles pulls up for a jumper that Cedric swats into the bleachers. Even with a bum knee, he can still sky.

Luther hits a long jumper, then misses a gimme at the foul line. Cedric rebounds and dribbles out to the top of the key. Luther picks him up, covers Cedric like a second skin, bumping him, contesting every dribble. Cedric brings the ball up to shoot. Luther slaps at the ball but only gets flesh. The ball doesn't even make it to the rim.

"My ball," says Cedric. "Got a foul."

Luther looks at him. "Bullshit."

Jo-Jo throws the ball back to Cedric.

"What you mean, Luther?" says Cedric. "You saying that handcuffing wasn't a foul?"

"Damn right," says Luther. "Quit crying."

Cedric bounces the ball to Luther.

"Okay, Luther, your ball."

Jo-Jo comes up to guard Luther, but Luther just holds it, looks over at Cedric.

"You afraid to guard me, superstar?"

Cedric just stares at him, puzzled but also a little pissed off. In high school Luther had been the point guard and Cedric the power forward. They'd been the two tightest guys on the team. Luther ran down loose balls, made a few steals, and hit a couple of jump shots, but the main reason he was on the court was to get Cedric the ball when he was close to the basket, even when Cedric was double-teamed. And he had. He'd gotten Cedric the ball enough for Cliffside High to win the state 2-A championship our senior year.

"Okay, Luther," Cedric says. "I'll guard you."

Luther passes the ball to Charles, gets it back, and spins toward the basket. He gets himself between Cedric and the goal, but when Luther releases the ball Cedric blocks it from behind, comes up with the loose ball, and dribbles out to the key. Luther's all over him but it doesn't matter. Cedric puts the ball between his legs one time, lines up the basket with his elbow, and releases.

The ball arcs toward the basket, so high you don't think it's ever coming down, and then it does, touching nothing but net. He does that four straight times, and for a few moments it's like all the bad things have been wiped away—the five-million-dollar contract he'd snorted up his nose, the injury, the arrests. It's like his sophomore year in high school again, that first game of the season, when nobody really knew how good Cedric was because he'd just played JV ball his freshman year. He'd scored thirty-seven points in that game, going head-to-head with a guy who was supposed to be the best player in the conference. We'd all felt good that night, not just for Cedric but for ourselves because he was one of us. We'd been in school together since the first grade. His daddy worked at the same mill as Luther's daddy and mine.

Later, after high school, after I'd started working construction, I'd watch him play on TV, first college, then pro. And it was like watching Cedric play made it easier to go into work the next morning, just having known him. The guys I worked with— Luther, Jo-Jo, all the ones who'd gone to school with him—they were like me. They watched the games on TV, checked the box scores in the newspaper. We'd talk about the games at lunch break, what Cedric had done the night before. Any maybe some of the guys were jealous, especially after he signed the five-million-dollar contract, but if they were I never heard it. We were proud of him, like he was our own flesh and blood.

After the fourth shot, Luther chests up to Cedric even more, so close you couldn't slip a piece of toilet paper between them. "That all you got?" he says to Cedric. Then again, "That all you got?"

Cedric gets the ball and doesn't even bother to fake. He just holds Luther off with his right arm and heads for the basket. I'm under the goal and I jump when Cedric jumps but I'm not even in the same time zone. Then before he can jam the ball through the net Luther cuts Cedric's legs out from under him. Cedric lands hard on his back. Then it's like nobody's breathing.

Cedric gets up slow, making sure he's not hurt.

Luther's next to him, the ball in his hands. "You want a foul, superstar?"

Cedric's up now, and Luther's not backing, so I get between them.

"Get out of my way," Luther tells me. "This ain't got nothing to do with you."

He doesn't add "because you're white," but that's what he's saying. And it's bullshit. When Cedric first started losing his game and you kept hearing about him missing practices, taking himself out after the first quarter, some of the guys at work, guys who'd know, said it was drugs. It was Luther and me who kept telling them no way, that Cedric was too smart to screw up what he had going. Even later, when the rumors weren't rumors anymore, we kept believing it was just a matter of time before he got his act together.

"I don't need this shit," Cedric says. He turns from Luther and walks over to the bleachers to get his sweat suit and gym bag. Then he disappears out the door.

Charles comes up to Luther. "What's the matter with you?" he asks. Then Charles walks over to the bleachers and picks up his sweats. The rest of us follow.

In the truck Luther pops the top on one of the Millers.

"Sorry I lost my cool," he says, handing me the beer.

I take it, but I'm not about to let a warm beer and a half-assed apology end it.

"You don't think I understand what was going down with you and Cedric? You don't think it has anything to do with me?"

Luther doesn't say anything for a minute. He's looking out the window. I remember how hard Cedric worked in high school, shooting free throws after practice, running dirt roads in the summer, lifting weights. But Luther and me had worked just as hard. We'd stayed after practice, run the dirt roads every day in the summer, lifted weights. We'd won the hustle awards, paid the price. Nobody practiced or played harder, but Luther didn't have the size and I didn't have the talent to go beyond high school. Only Cedric had that.

Luther turns and looks at me. He meets my eyes for a second, long enough.

"Yeah," he says. "You're a part of it."

THE CABLE COMPANY hasn't unhooked my cable for nonpayment yet, so as soon as I get home, I shower, heat up some leftover chicken, and turn on TBS. The Hawks are playing the Bulls. The announcers are talking about how great Jordan is, swearing nobody has even come close to him. Maybe I'm wrong but I'm not seeing anything Cedric didn't do eight, maybe ten years ago. Maybe not as flashy as Jordan, but close, damn close.

I get tired of hearing the announcers, so I turn down the sound and put my scratched-to-hell copy of *Eat a Peach* on the turntable.

The first notes of "One Way Out" blast out of the speakers. More ghosts. Ole Duane Allman, playing that slide guitar like he knew he wouldn't be around long. Berry Oakley, dead now as well. Gregg Allman, who tried his damndest to join them but is still around. I saw him last April in Charlotte. He looked like he'd just been paroled from hell, but he could still sing and bang the piano. They say he's clean now, so maybe some people do get a second chance. By the time the album ends I'm too tired to get up and turn it over. I close my eyes.

When I wake up the game is over. I'm not sure how long I've slept but it's long enough to have a dream, a dream about Cedric.

We're in high school and Cedric's playing ball again, the way he used to, no bloodshot eyes, no knee brace. He swoops in from the foul line for a dunk and we are all watching, me and my daddy and momma, and Luther's daddy and momma, and our brothers and sisters, and Luther's kids. Everything is in slow motion. Cedric keeps gliding toward the basket, and we start shouting, screaming, and praying he won't ever come down.

❖

Cold Harbor

She did not dream about him. Anna dreamed about the others, the ones who died. They came at night and lay beside her, crowding the bed, pressing their cold bodies against her. She'd wake trembling, turn her face toward the night-light that lit the lower wall. She would lie there, her eyes open, and this was when she'd think of Josh Triplett.

They had brought him in on a heavy day of fighting, the helicopter descending slow as a vulture each time it delivered a fresh supply of torn flesh and shattered bones. He was so slick with blood they used their fingers as much as their eyes to find the wounds. It was early in her tour of duty, early enough that she could still be amazed at how much blood a body held. She and the doctor found four wounds, one that mangled his arm, one in the neck, two lesser ones in his chest. They stanched the wounds, but his blood pressure still dropped.

Anna had been the one who unlaced his boots, the right one pouring blood when she pulled it off and found the fifth wound, a slashed artery above the ankle.

"This lady saved your life, soldier," the doctor told him the next day as they stopped at his bed during their rounds. Private Triplett looked up from the cot and raised his hand and she held it. He squeezed her fingers, tears welling in his eyes. The throat wound kept him from speaking, but his mouth formed a thank you.

"I can write your family, let them know you're okay. Do you want me to do that?" she asked.

Triplett nodded, freed his hand, and pointed to the pen in the doctor's shirt pocket. Across the doctor's pad he scrawled,

Mrs. Lawson Triplett
Aho Creek Road
Route 4
Boone, North Carolina

"I'll write her tonight," she said.

When she came back the next morning he was gone, helicoptered to the 311th station hospital, where he would begin his rehabilitation.

That was two years ago. Anna couldn't remember what he looked like except he had gray eyes. It seemed so wrong to her that she remembered the faces of the dead more clearly than one who had lived.

Dawn filtered through the one window in her apartment, and though it was Saturday she did not try to drift back to sleep. She left the bed where she'd lain awake the last hour, the bed she'd slept in alone the last three months. She opened the dresser drawer and read the letter from Josh Triplett's mother.

Dear Miss Bradley,
Thank you for looking after my son and thank you for letting me know he is all right. God bless you and all others helping save our boys.

Sincerely,
Edith Triplett

On the envelope was the address she'd memorized. She ate quickly and showered. Then came the hardest thing, deciding what to wear. She finally chose a navy blue skirt and blouse her husband had given her their one Christmas together. She already knew which roads to take, had mapped the route weeks ago.

There was one more thing to do before leaving. She found the note he'd mailed with the papers and dialed the number. The phone rang five times before Jonathon's groggy voice answered.

"I've signed the papers," she said.

"I'll come by and get them or you can mail them back," Jonathon said.

"I'll mail them back."

"Anna," he said. "Call the VA. They've got doctors, psychiatrists. They might be able to help you."

"So you think I'm crazy."

"I didn't say that."

She hung up the phone.

Anna picked up her purse and the atlas. Midafternoon and I'll be there, she guessed, glancing at the clock as she walked to the door. Whether Josh Triplett would be there she did not know. A phone call could have answered this question, but she didn't want him to know she was coming. If they met again, it would be just like the first time—suddenly, with no time for calculated responses but instead a gesture from the heart, like that morning he'd raised his hand to hold hers.

SHE WAS OUT of Washington by six-thirty, passing through Alexandria, where she'd grown up. Few cars were on the road as she drove south into the hilly region where so many battles had been fought a century earlier. The blue and white signs raised at the highway's edge listed them. Manassas, Fredericksburg, Chancellorsville, and Spotsylvania recalled wide, deep-green pastures she'd visited on school field trips, Saturday excursions with her parents. These outings had always been fun, the dead mere numbers on metal and stone. It was only after Korea that she found it obscene that people could picnic, play softball and football on ground where men had shed their blood.

She stopped outside of Richmond at a store across the highway from Cold Harbor, the battlefield where Grant had lost seven thousand men in eight minutes. While an attendant filled the Studebaker with gas and cleaned the windshield, Anna walked inside the cinder-block building. Paintings of gray- and blue-clad soldiers filled the wall behind the cash register, orange price tags taped to the corners. Raised sabers and tattered flags jabbed the tops of paintings, below them men gripping muskets. As she waited for her change, Anna remembered what she'd learned in high school about Cold Harbor, how the night before battle Union soldiers sat by their campfires and pinned names and hometowns on the backs of their uniforms, knowing better than their commander what the morning would bring. She wondered how many of these paintings would sell if they depicted men whose faces had been torn from their heads, men whose intestines spilled from their bodies like some pink stew. Things she'd seen and knew would have occurred in the 1860s as well, for though the weapons were more efficient now the results had always been the same.

South of Petersburg she turned west, passing through Appomattox and Roanoke and Radford, the land growing less inhabited, more stark and mountainous as she turned south again, following the New River deeper into the Appalachians. The oldest mountains in the world, the road atlas claimed. She soon passed a green sign that said WELCOME TO NORTH CAROLINA.

She stopped in Boone, refilled the Studebaker with gas, bought a Coke and plastic-wrapped sandwich for lunch. She asked the man who took her money for directions to Aho Creek Road, and the man took out a pen and scribbled on a napkin.

"That's a far-back place where you're headed," the man said, handing her the napkin. "You got kin up there?"

"No," Anna said, "friends."

Twenty minutes later she turned onto Aho Creek Road, plumes of dust rising in her rearview mirror as she drove up the mountain, slowing to read the names on the mailboxes—Hampton, Greene,

Watson—then a white clapboard church, a few dozen tombstones jutting out of the ground like snaggled teeth. A hundred yards farther was a dented mailbox brown with rust, the red flag leaning like a semaphore. Triplett. Anna turned in to a rutted driveway that did not so much end as fade into a front yard.

She glanced in the mirror, decided not to put on more lipstick, then got out, walking across the yard and up the farmhouse's stone steps. Her hand shook as she raised it, paused, then rapped her knuckles against the wood. No sound came from inside. She knocked again, harder.

Anna heard footsteps and caught a glimpse of a gray eye behind a curtain.

"What do you want?" a woman's voice asked.

"My name is Anna Bradley."

The door remained unopened. No muffled reply came from the other side.

"I wrote you two years ago, Mrs. Triplett. I was your son's nurse."

The door opened halfway, but the woman did not step out, half of her face hidden as she spoke.

"What do you want?" Mrs. Triplett asked again.

"I came to see Josh, to see how he's getting along. I thought you could tell me how he's doing, where he is now."

"He's out yonder," Mrs. Triplett said, nodding toward the pasture, the church spire that rose beyond it.

For a terrible moment Anna thought the old woman meant the cemetery.

"He's got him a trailer in the pasture there," she said and

opened the door a little wider, jabbed her finger out. "Down there in the hollow. You go down there. You'll see how he's doing."

She waited for Mrs. Triplett to say something else, but the old woman offered no more words, so Anna turned and stepped off the porch. It was windier and colder here than it had been in Washington, the air stingier, like Korea. She straddled the barbed-wire fence carefully so as not to tear her skirt. Anna wished she'd worn pants and a coat as she followed a creek through the pasture and into the hollow, her breath rapid though the land sloped downhill.

After a hundred yards the decline steepened. A scarecrow dressed in a helmet and camouflage rose up before her, a Purple Heart pinned at the center of the empty chest. The scarecrow's seed sack face was featureless except for an unlipped grin and two black, filled-in circles where eyes might have been, its arms stretched wide as if to embrace her. For the first time in her journey she thought of turning back.

Beyond the scarecrow's arms Anna saw the trailer's roof and skinny chimney, wisps of smoke rising from it. She stepped around the scarecrow, more of the gray Airstream trailer visible with each step into the hollow—first the uncurtained window, then the door with no steps leading up to it, finally the rotting tires sagging into the ground.

The metal door swung open before she could knock. A tall, gaunt man filled the doorway. He wore overalls and a flannel shirt the same color as his eyes, the empty sleeve's cuff pinned to the shoulder. He loomed above her, the look on his face unfathomable. Wind rustled the empty sleeve. Like a flag, Anna thought.

She saw the stoma where the laryngectomy had been performed. The only sounds were the whisper of the wind in the trees, the gurgle of the creek as it flowed past the trailer.

"Do you remember me?" she asked.

He nodded. His neck quivered, a quick gulping of air into the esophagus, then a low, harsh burp of words.

"Why are you here?"

"I wanted to see you, to see how you were getting along."

He swallowed.

"Now you've seen me."

Anna did not move.

"What else do you want?" Josh Triplett said.

Anna wanted to tell him what she felt the night Jonathon, who'd never been in a war, asked "Why can't you just be happy, happy that a bad time in your life is over with?" Anna wanted to tell Josh Triplett she once believed that after a while the world would return to what it was before Korea, that time could fade what she'd seen the same way it faded a photograph left out in light. She wanted to tell him that she'd once saved his life and now she needed him to help save hers.

"I have dreams," she finally said. "Dreams about the men I saw die."

He spoke, each clot of words followed by a quick swallow.

"I have dreams too, I dream of before, when I had two arms, when people didn't, look away when I spoke." He pulled a handkerchief from his pocket, wiped spittle from the stoma.

"But you're not dead," she said, her voice quivering.

"Sometimes I wonder if I really am alive," he said.

"You're alive," she said.

"Then maybe I shouldn't be."

Anna leaned against the trailer, tried to blink away the tears as Josh Triplett looked down at her, his gray eyes unblinking as a hawk's.

"You saved my life," he said. "I know that. Maybe I'll be glad you did. Someday."

His words passed over her like cloud shadow, a cloud whose color is unknown. There was no inflection to tell if his words were sarcastic or compassionate.

As Anna walked out of the hollow she remembered the note left on the bed the day Jonathon left.

"I want a future," the note said.

Mrs. Triplett waited on the porch.

"Come inside and warm up," she said.

Anna was too weary to say no, so she stepped onto the porch and followed Mrs. Triplett into the front room, whose only light came from the fireplace. The old woman dragged a ladder-back chair in front of the fire and led her to it, then disappeared into the back of the house. She brought back a tin cup filled with coffee.

"Drink this," Mrs. Triplett said.

Anna shivered so violently she held the cup with both hands, afraid to raise it to her face lest she spill it. The cup warmed her palms as she closed her eyes, leaned her face toward the fire and let it bathe her in its heat. The old woman stood close by, saying nothing. When Anna quit shaking she brought the cup to her mouth, her eyes still closed, imagining the coffee a warm glow as it moved down her throat into her belly. She sipped and listened to the crackle of the fire, the ticking of the clock on the mantelpiece. Warm now, she leaned back in the chair and for a few minutes slept without dreaming as the fire's heat covered her like a quilt.

The clock chimed five times and Anna opened her eyes. The cup was still in her hands, but all that remained were a few grounds sloshing the bottom.

"You want more?"

"No, no thank you," Anna said. "I've got to be going."

"How far you got to go?"

"Washington," she said.

"You could spend the night here. I've got an extra bed."

"No, I need to go," Anna said, getting up from the chair.

The old woman looked into the fire, her palms held out to its warmth.

"My sister's son, he got polio when he was eight. Somehow they got through that. My brother, he fought the Japanese during the World War. He come back home and you'd not know he'd left. He went back to farming and got on with his life. It made me believe people could endure about anything. I don't know that to be true anymore."

"I don't either," Anna said.

"Some grief is like barbed wire that's been wrapped around a tree," Mrs. Triplett said. "The longer it's there the deeper the barbs go, the closer to the tree's heart."

Mrs. Triplett took the cup from Anna's hand, placed it on the mantel.

"It's kind of you to come," she said. "I should have been friendlier when you first showed up. What's happened to Josh, it's done made me bitter."

"I understand," Anna said.

"Do you have children?"

"No."

"That's a shame," Mrs. Triplett said, her hands held again to the fire. "You have a good heart. You'd be a good mother."

Anna shook her head.

"No, I wouldn't be."

Anna turned and walked on out to her car. Through the windshield she saw Mrs. Triplett's face in a window. The old woman raised a hand in front of her weathered face, her palm open as if offering a blessing.

Anna backed out of the driveway and started down the mountain toward Boone, the sun already sunk behind the mountains. She would drive as far as she could. When the road began to blur and she was too tired to go on, she would stop at a motel.

By then she would have crossed the Virginia line, driven through Pulaski and Roanoke and Lynchburg, the land leveling out as she skirted the lower Shenandoah Valley. Somewhere among the old killing fields between Appomattox and Manassas she would find a crossroads or hamlet with a name drenched in history. She'd be too exhausted to eat or take a shower. She would take off her shoes, blouse, and skirt and slip on her nightgown. Anna would turn on the bathroom light and pull back the covers, close her eyes and remember the warmth of fire and coffee as she lay down again with the dead.

❖

Honesty

I met Lee Ann McIntyre on a date suggested by my wife. Kelly always read the personals as she drank her morning coffee. "Better than the comics," she said and would read aloud the ads she found most amusing.

"Why not an article about what it's like to meet your soul partner through a newspaper ad," she said one June morning as we sat at the kitchen table. "You go out on the date and write about it. That could be amusing."

"I don't think so," I replied.

I looked out the wide bay window where our cat stalked a chipmunk.

"I think it's a very good idea," Kelly said, and trailing her words like a shadow was the fact that my book *The Myth of Robert Frost* was stillborn at thirty-eight pages. I looked at her, dressed administratively in her dark blue blazer and skirt while I was barefoot, clothed in jeans and a T-shirt. Unlike me, she had somewhere to go, something to do.

"I've even got a woman picked out for you," she said, holding up the paper between us. "Let's deconstruct this, darling. 'Hopelessly Lonely.' Now would that be the signifier or the signified? No matter. 'DWF, 32, brown/green, 5-6, 140.' No mention of whether she still has any teeth. 'Likes mountains, quiet evenings, and reading.' See, you all are a perfect match, though you better bone up on Harlequin romances. 'Seeks WM, 25–40.' What did I tell you? That's you exactly, it's fate. 'A knight in shining armor.' We'll have to work on that. 'Who likes children.' You like children, don't you? How about three or four. This woman probably has them. 'And understands the hardships of life.' You understand the hardships of life, don't you?"

Kelly took a pen from her briefcase.

"Here," she said, circling the ad. "Call *Carolina Tempo*. I guarantee they'll go for this idea. Then call Hopelessly Lonely. Leave a message that you want to take her to dinner at the Grey Pheasant. Tell her knights in shining armor don't take their dates to Wendy's or the Waffle House. That will put you ahead of the rest of the guys who call."

"You're not worried I might fall in love and leave you?" I said.

"No," Kelly said, her smile much larger than mine. "I'm not worried about that at all."

After Kelly left I took the newspaper into the den, what Kelly called my "writing room." Like taking a year's leave from teaching to write full-time, the room had been her idea. She'd been the one who picked out the bookcases, the huge oak desk, the new computer and printer. I sat down where I sat every morning, sipping coffee, sharpening pencils, looking out the window, doing everything a writer does but write.

I reread the first chapter of my book, thirty-eight pages of jargon and endnotes, just as tedious and silly as they were nine months earlier, when I wrote them. I pushed the manuscript to the table's far edge as if it were some dead creature beginning to smell. I looked at a notebook page filled with ideas for articles, trying to find one that Larry Kendrick might like better than Kelly's.

"I like the newspaper date idea," Larry said when I called him an hour later.

"What about the old poverty in the New South article?"

"Look," Larry said. "This isn't *The Daily Worker*."

"Okay," I said.

A year earlier I wouldn't have done it, but I had only three more months to come up with something to justify my year off. At least the article would be some sort of publication, even if in a magazine no one outside North Carolina had ever heard of.

By now I knew Kelly expected me to fail, had set up the room, the free time as a way of showing me that I was nothing more than what she'd known me to be all along, an actor who mouthed the clichés and jargon of others because he had no words of his own. That was the way she saw me, and that was the way she wanted me to see myself, stripped bare of props and pretense.

I picked up the phone and dialed the number in the newspaper, then the four digits after the circled ad. I heard the same message

Kelly had read, but this time *g*'s left off endings, words stretched into extra syllables. I left my first name and phone number and said that I hadn't ridden a horse in years, but I'd try to be a knight in shining armor. I told her I'd like to take her to the Grey Pheasant, a restaurant worthy of a princess. I played my role well.

I sat back down at the desk with no idea when, or if, my message would be returned. In the distance the college's clock tower rose stern and gray above late May green. Three more months and I'd be back there, disabused of any notions of what I had to offer the world.

Kelly was home when Lee Ann McIntyre called.

"You get it," Kelly said. "It might be your princess."

"Is this Richard?" a woman asked, her voice doubtful, though whether about the number or about this whole venture was unclear. Kelly was in the other room, but I knew she listened.

"Yes," I said.

"I liked your message," Lee Ann McIntyre said. "I liked what you said, how you said it."

"So you want to go out?" I asked.

"Yes," she said, her voice soft, still a little doubtful. "I think that would be nice."

"So what did you arrange?" Kelly asked when I hung up.

"She works Friday and Saturday, so we're going out Sunday night."

"What else?" Kelly asked.

"Her name is Lee Ann McIntyre."

"And she lives where?"

"Out on Highway Eight."

"In a trailer, of course. No one named Lee Ann lives in a house."

"Yes," I said. "What of it?"

"The knight defends his princess," Kelly said.

"This is a bad idea," I said. "It could be cruel too."

"You have an exaggerated sense of your charisma," Kelly said. "She'll be just as bored with you as you are with her. You're giving her a free meal at a restaurant where they wouldn't even let her waitress. That's a good deal if you ask me."

"This woman's got enough problems without my adding to them," I said.

"You mean 'the hard considerations of the poor,' " Kelly said. "Though of course you argued Wharton was upholding the power structure even as she made that statement." Kelly smiled. "See, I remember something from your class."

I got up to go into my office.

"Why is it writers sentimentalize the poor?" Kelly asked. "And I mean a real answer, not some Marxist cliché."

"Maybe because a lot of them didn't grow up as privileged as you."

"Or you, Mr. Prep School," Kelly said. "It's funny, isn't it, how people used to be ashamed of being born poor and now they're ashamed of coming from wealth."

"I don't sense it ever bothered you," I said.

"Why should it? I'm glad my parents were wealthy. I'm glad I am too."

I met her eyes.

"Why did you marry me?"

"Because you needed me, silly," Kelly said and smiled the same tight smile I remembered from the evening three years earlier when she'd sat in on my class.

The college had instituted a "Knowing Each Other Better" program that year for faculty and administration, an effort, as our president put it, to narrow the divide between the two. There had been several receptions as well as visits of administrators to faculty classes. Kelly, who was associate dean of academic affairs, had attended my American literature class.

She was ten minutes late, her plaid skirt and black blazer a sharp contrast to the proletariat uniform of jeans and work shirts I and most of the class wore. She sat on the front row, a supercilious smile on her face. I continued with my lecture, trying not to be distracted by the presence of a woman who might be involved in deciding which faculty were let go during the college's next budget crisis.

I was talking about Frost's "Death of the Hired Man," explaining how the poem's seeming sympathy for the downtrodden ultimately reinforced the hegemonic structure of society. The students had been responsive, good questions and comments. Kelly said nothing, her lips pursed in a tight smile I found more and more disconcerting as the period passed.

She did not leave her seat until the rest of the class had gone.

"Did I pass the audition?" I asked, an ironic smile on my face to match hers.

"Maybe," she said. "That's not the kind of thing we discussed in my lit classes at Bennington. There it was all scanning lines and looking for archetypes."

"That's the problem with small liberal arts colleges," I said.

"It wasn't until grad school at Duke that I saw literature had some connection to the real world."

I'd realize later Kelly sensed I was about to launch into a lengthy anecdote about my conversion at Duke, so she cut me off in midsentence.

"Do you have plans for the evening, Professor?" she asked.

"Just a few student essays to grade."

"Well, how about I buy you a drink at the Grey Pheasant? Let the essays wait a while."

"That would be nice," I said.

I followed her taillights to the restaurant. We parked and then walked into the bar the college's employees shared with the town's other professionals.

"I picked your class to attend for a reason," Kelly said, handing me my drink. "We met at the dean's party last fall. You don't remember me there, of course."

I didn't. Kelly is an attractive woman but there's not that one feature—lush lips, high cheekbones—that makes an immediate impression.

"You were holding forth about the rigors of academic life. It sounded pretty pretentious, especially to someone who sees how empty the faculty parking lot is by midafternoon. But I could see you had potential. Nice eyes too."

Kelly placed her hand on top of mine and I did not withdraw it. She was, after all, my superior. I wasn't tenured and didn't need any enemies in administration. But it was more than that. I liked her cynicism, the mockery in her voice and eyes, how she viewed *everything* the way I viewed literature. I wanted to match her cynicism, and I did. I matched it enough to marry her.

ON SUNDAY EVENING I bumped up the washed-out driveway to Lee Ann McIntyre's trailer, parking behind a decade-old Ford Escort with a smashed rear fender. A couple of leafless saplings wilted in the front yard, no more alive than sticks jabbed in the ground. An orange and blue plastic tricycle was wedged under the trailer, a saggy beach ball beside the concrete steps.

I knocked on the screen door, and the voice I'd heard on the phone told me to come in.

"I'll be out in a second," Lee Ann McIntyre said. "Have a seat."

I sat on the couch. Across from me a playpen bulged with bright, cheap toys, above it a picture of three kids sitting at a picnic table, in the corner a TV and a plastic bookshelf filled with paperbacks, books with "Desire" and "Passion" in their titles.

"I'm ready," she said, and I looked away from the books.

Lee Ann McIntyre stood in the doorway that led to the rest of her trailer. She wore black high heels, a dark blue dress, probably what she'd worn that morning if she'd gone to church. Her hair was blond, too long for a face that had aged quickly—maybe from too much sun, maybe from too many kids too soon. But there had been a time when she was pretty, I could see that.

"Where are your kids?" I asked. "I'd like to meet them."

She blushed, as if they'd been a secret she'd hoped to keep from me.

"They're at my sister's."

I waited a few seconds, but she offered no drink, no small talk. She had her pocketbook in her hand as if she couldn't wait to get out of the trailer.

We didn't say much in the car. I asked about her children, but she didn't warm to the subject. Maybe she thought I was prying, or maybe she was so exhausted from raising three kids alone she wanted a few minutes without having to think about them. I asked who she liked to read and that got us to town without too many more long pauses.

Inside the Grey Pheasant, the maître d' led us past the bar where Kelly and I had come three years ago after my class. He seated us in the corner opposite the bar, and it made me a little nervous, because sometimes faculty members came in for an evening drink. I sat facing away from the bar and the mirror that filled the wall behind it.

I ordered a gin and tonic and Lee Ann said she'd take the same. I drank mine and ordered another, while she stirred her drink with the red straw as if searching for something in it, only occasionally taking a sip. She was nervous and seemed suspicious as well.

We both ordered filet mignon, and when she'd finished her drink she opened up a little more, telling me about the upper part of the county where'd she had grown up, where I went trout fishing some days when I tired of pretending to be a writer. She knew the places I fished, and that seemed to make me more credible. Our salads came and she ate with more relish than I did. She asked if I had kids, and when I said no she seemed to assume that meant I'd never been married. She talked more about her children, how the oldest, who was only ten, was already boy crazy and how that bothered her.

"I married at eighteen," she said. "I don't want her making the same mistake."

"How long have you been divorced?" I asked.

"Two years."

"Does your ex-husband help with the children?"

Lee Ann laughed humorlessly.

"No."

"Why not?" I asked.

"He's in prison."

She didn't look down at her drink when she said it or act embarrassed. Her tone was matter-of-fact.

"He's in prison?" I said. "Prison?"

"At least until next February."

"What did he do?" I asked.

Lee Ann hesitated. "He tried to kill me."

She must have thought I didn't believe that either, because she pulled back her hair. A welt long and thick as a cigarette purpled her neck. But it wasn't a welt. It was a scar, a scar that hadn't healed right, or maybe covered a wound so deep and ragged it could never heal right. As I stared at the scar the restaurant became bright and strange, as if, until that moment, I had been someplace else, someplace far away. I was the one looking at my drink now.

"That's why I need a knight in shining armor," she said, her laugh brittle. "To get me away from here, away from North Carolina, someplace where he can't find me when he's out."

Lee Ann paused. Her right hand lay beside the silverware. She moved her thumb and index finger so they touched the knife's handle.

"He swore he'd kill me when he got out," she said, looking right at me.

"People say all sorts of things," I said. "They're just words."

I wasn't sure who I was trying to convince.

Lee Ann just shook her head.

"You don't know him."

She started to say something more, then decided not to speak. A man wearing a jacket and tie passed our table, but it wasn't anyone I knew.

"What is it?" I asked. "You can tell me."

"You know what I pray?" she said, and I shook my head. "I pray he doesn't do it in front of the children."

She didn't say anything else and I didn't either. In a couple of minutes the waiter brought our main course. He placed two stemmed glasses next to our silverware, then lifted an ice bucket from the cart, in it a bottle of champagne.

"I don't understand," I said. "I didn't order this."

"Compliments of the lady," the waiter said, nodding toward the entrance. "The whole meal is."

Kelly sat at the far end of the bar. I had no idea how long she'd been there, but I could see her wineglass was almost empty as she raised it in a toast to me, to Lee Ann.

I looked in the bar's mirror and saw the back of Kelly's head, saw what she saw—two people who needed a lesson in reality, and she was willing to foot the bill to make that lesson possible.

"Who is she?" Lee Ann asked, suspicion in her voice.

"My wife," I said.

"I should have known this wasn't right," Lee Ann said. Her voice was as soft as when she told me she expected to be killed.

I thought she would start crying. She looked like she might, but she didn't. She'd probably learned long ago how useless tears were.

Kelly was still at the bar, watching us.

"I want to go home," Lee Ann said, and I didn't argue.

I didn't look Kelly's way as we went out, and we were almost back to Lee Ann's trailer before I tried to apologize.

"Was my ad so stupid you thought you could do this to me?" she asked.

"No," I said.

"Was it some kind of joke?"

I shook my head.

"Why then?"

"Because I was unhappy with my marriage. I wanted to be with someone else awhile," I said, and that was a lie, and I didn't care. I'd had enough truth for a while, and I believed Lee Ann had as well.

She looked out the window at the yards flashing past, some with children playing in the last light.

"He sends me pictures he draws," she said. "Pictures of me with just my head, no body. My eyes are open in those pictures. My mouth too. I'm screaming. He calls them Valentines."

She closed her eyes and I said nothing. I didn't want to know what she was thinking.

When we got back to the trailer Lee Ann unbuckled her seat belt but didn't get out. I reached for my door handle but she touched my arm.

"Would you hold me?" she asked. "Please, just for a few moments."

I placed my arm around her, awkward as a high school kid on a first date, but that didn't seem to matter. She laid her cheek against my chest. We didn't say anything. We just sat there as the dark deepened around us. After a while her sister drove up with the kids, and I walked her to the trailer's battered door. I drove back home to a life where all that was required of me was that I look in the mirror from time to time.

I DIDN'T DO the article for *Carolina Tempo,* and I threw the thirty-eight pages of *The Myth of Robert Frost* in the trash can Kelly had so thoughtfully made a part of my writing room. The next time Kelly asked what I was working on, I handed her my course syllabi for the fall. She read each one carefully before handing them back.

"You've finally found your voice," she said.

I don't know what happened to Lee Ann McIntyre. Probably she left North Carolina long before her husband got out of prison, but every time the newspaper has a story about a local murder I quickly turn the page, afraid I'll see her face staring back at me. But I do think of her quite often. What I remember most about my date with Lee Ann McIntyre was standing with her outside the trailer afterward. The night air was muggy and still, and somewhere back in the woods an owl called.

"Somehow, despite all this, I still think you're a good person," she said.

She took my hand, and I felt the warmth of her flesh touching mine, and I could almost believe, for a brief moment, that had we met at a different time and place we might even have fallen in love.

"No, I'm not," I said finally, and let her hand slip free from mine.

Dangerous Love

When Ricky threw his knife and the blade tore my blouse and cut into flesh eight inches from my heart, it was certain as the blood trickling down my arm that something in our relationship had gone wrong.

"Cut the rest of it off," a townie in a yellow ball cap yelled from the bleachers, thinking ripping my blouse was part of the show.

"Work on that dress some too," said a man on the front row.

Another townie stepped through the tent entrance and sat down.

"What have I missed?" he asked.

"Near about a execution," the man behind him said.

Twenty feet in front of me, Ricky stared at his empty right hand like he was holding it out for Lady Socrates to tell his future. But Lady Socrates was three tents down the midway. Ricky would have to figure it out on his own what his hand told him. The folks in the stands started whistling and yelling but Ricky just kept staring at his hand. I wondered if he saw his future in the lifeline that crossed his palm. I wondered if he saw a future that included me.

"Don't waste your money on such as that," Momma had said that first night, but it was my dollar bill. I'd earned it waiting on smart alecks and grumps, coming home every night with aching feet and smelling like grease and cigarettes. All that for minimum wage and a few quarters thrown on the counter.

I stared at the painting on the tent, the figure of a gypsy-looking woman with so many knives jutting out around her she looked to be sprouting quills like a porcupine. The knife thrower had his hand behind his ear, ready to hurl another knife. He wore a droopy mustache, his long hair flowing down his back. RICARDO MONT BLANC: WORLD-FAMOUS KNIFE THROWER, the caption said.

"I'm going," I told Momma and handed the woman at the ticket booth my dollar.

The light was shadowy inside. The air smelled of sawdust and sweat. Five rows of half-filled bleachers filled one side of the tent. At the back a piece of plywood stood like a knobless door. A human outline had been drawn on the wood, like on police shows when somebody's been killed. I sat down in the first row, the only woman in the audience.

A man opened the flap at the back of the tent, what looked like a wooden suitcase in his left hand. He was blonder than I'd expected from the poster and name, so handsome with his green eyes and long, wavy hair. He wore all black from shirt to boots. Younger than I'd supposed too, his brow unlined and mustache fine as peach fuzz. I reckoned he was about my age, still in his mid-twenties.

The knife thrower opened the carrying case. There was nothing inside but black-handled knives with long, bright blades— beautiful, deadly looking knives. He didn't say a word, just picked one up and flung it. The knife made a loud whack as it entered the plywood, the blade no more than an inch above the outline's right wrist. He flung another, hitting the same exact spot, except this time above the left wrist.

"Where's your damsel in distress?" a pimply-faced young rowdy yelled from the row behind me.

"Don't have one," Ricardo Mont Blanc said and threw another knife, which landed between the outline's legs.

"I figured there to be a pretty woman for you to throw at," the teenager said.

"It ain't nothing to throw at a piece of plywood," an old man on the top row added. "There ain't no risk to that."

"Then you get up there," Ricardo Mont Blanc said. "I'll throw at you."

"I'd be more than enough willing, but the doctor says I can't do nothing that excites me. Bad ticker," the geezer said, pointing to his chest.

"Anyway, he ain't pretty enough," the teenager said. "Why don't you put her up there?"

I didn't need to turn around to know who he was talking about.

The man sitting next to me nudged my shoulder. "Get on up there, girl," he said. "Give us something worth looking at."

Some of the other men echoed his words and I could feel a blush spreading across my face.

"That girl ain't got the grit to get up there," the old man said. "I'm getting my money back."

I looked at him and I knew exactly the kind of customer he'd be. He'd hog a whole booth instead of sitting on a stool and order just coffee and make sure you ran your legs off to keep it hot and up to the brim. He'd sit there an hour and then grumble when he got the bill that seventy-five cents was too much for coffee. There'd be as much chance of a tip from him as from an alley cat.

"I'll let him throw at me," I said, knowing me standing in front of that plywood would keep that geezer from getting his dollar back. But it was more than that. I wanted to show Ricardo Mont Blanc that I did have grit.

The tent got real quiet soon as the words left my mouth.

Ricardo Mont Blanc aimed those cool green eyes right at me. Sizing me up, I reckoned. I mostly expected him to say something such as he couldn't throw at just anyone or there might be a problem with the carnival's insurance or some other excuse like that.

All he said was "Okay."

"We got us a show now," the young rowdy shouted and high-fived another teenager sitting next to him.

Ricardo Mont Blanc led me over to the plywood. He fitted me inside the outline, raising my arms, positioning my head. His hands were soft, not rough and callused like most men's hands. I couldn't help but wonder how they'd feel touching other places on my body. But another part of me was all the while looking for the slightest tremble in them.

"What's your name?" he asked when he had me like he wanted.

"Ellie Higginbotham," I said.

"Call me Ricky," he said and took a step back, looked me over a last time.

"Don't move, Ellie Higginbotham," he said and walked to the other side of the tent.

Momma had always said I was bad to do things without thinking them through, like after high school marrying Robert instead of taking a scholarship Brevard College offered me. I closed my eyes. Dear Lord, my mother was so right, I prayed. Forgive my foolishness and let me leave this tent alive. I said a silent amen and looked up. Ricky's eyes met mine. He gave a little nod. My eyes locked on his as his arm came forward.

"YOU AIN'T THOUGHT this thing through, no more than when you turned down that scholarship," Momma said four days later as Daddy drove me to the fairgrounds. "You could be teaching school now instead of having knives thrown at you."

"I don't know as I could trust a man with a name nobody in South Carolina's heard the like of," Daddy chimed in.

"That's not his real name, Daddy," I said. "His real name's Ricky Sandifer."

"And what does that tell you, him disguising his name like that?" Daddy said. "Where do his parents live? Has he told you that?"

"They're dead, Daddy."

"So he claims," Daddy said. "I'm going to be checking those wanted posters in the post office, girl. You best be eyeballing them too."

"Even as a child, you always did things different," Momma said. "Your sisters would never run off with the circus."

"It's not a circus, Momma. It's a carnival."

"And that's worse," Daddy said. "Circus people are high society compared to the riffraff you'll be with."

"I've made up my mind," I said and lifted my suitcase from the floorboard.

Momma shook her head.

"That's what you said when we tried talking you out of marrying Robert," she said, "those exact same words. Those teachers of yours always bragged about how smart you were, but there's book smarts and life smarts, Ellie, and they ain't the same thing."

"It's different this time," I said.

NOW, SIX MONTHS later, I wasn't nearly so sure. I pulled the knife out of my blouse. The blade had nicked my upper arm, not muscle-deep but deep enough to sting and stain my blouse with blood.

I thought about what Momma said about me not thinking things through. I'd married Robert knowing no more about what holds a man and woman together than I'd known about being an astronaut. But in the years since I'd learned a lot about men and women and love—mostly about how those three things never seemed to make a good fit, at least for me. At eighteen I'd believed love was like a virus. If you stayed around someone, or better yet married him, sooner or later you'd catch it. And maybe love did happen that way for some people, but it hadn't for me, or at least the kind of love I wanted.

"You expect too much," my friend Connie told me after the divorce.

"I don't expect any more than I'm willing to give."

"Which is everything—heart, mind, body, and soul—nothing held back," Connie said. "That scares people, Ellie. It's too intense. It's like you want nothing between you and the other person, no skin, no muscle, just raw bone against raw bone."

Connie shook her head.

"Girl, if you don't learn to lower your expectations, you'll live a lonely life. There may be a man out there who wants that kind of intensity, has it himself, but he's one in a million. And even if you found him, how do you know that intensity won't be like a fire that burns up the both of you? That's a dangerous love you're talking about, Ellie Higginbotham."

BUT I HAD found that kind of love, found it that first night after Ricky'd thrown his knives at me and we'd bought a couple of corn dogs and Pepsis and sat on the steps of his camper. We'd talked easy and open with each other, and before long I was telling him things I'd never told Robert or even Momma. And it felt right to tell him those things, because I'd already trusted him with my heart in that tent. Unlike Robert and the other men I'd known, Ricky wanted to know everything about me. He wanted nothing hidden between us, even on that first night. It was like a hunger we shared, and soon enough he told me about his parents and sister, the car wreck that killed them. He told how he'd worked in the carnival since he was fifteen, first running a cotton candy machine, then working with the Snake Man, throwing knives every morning until he was good enough to earn a tent of his own. All the while he never tried to talk me into his camper and out of my clothes, even when the air got chilly and I snuggled against him.

It was dawn before I left. When I did Ricky knew more about me than Robert had in two years of marriage, more than Momma and Daddy in twenty-four years. I somehow knew myself better too, because different as our lives had been Ricky and me shared something deep inside and we'd shared it with each other for years and not even known. And it was more than how we saw life or how we lived life. It was how we felt life.

"You expect too much," Connie had said, and in the last four years I'd almost been convinced she was right, but that night on those camper steps I could finally believe she was wrong after all. When I said goodbye to Ricky that morning I knew I'd soon enough see the inside of that camper. I knew already when the carnival left Seneca I'd be leaving with it.

"THOSE TOWNIES DON'T ever come to see me do good," Ricky had said that night Momma and Daddy brought me to his camper, after I'd unpacked my suitcase, after we'd made love as the carnival's green and red and blue neon lights splashed across our bodies.

"They'd like nothing better than to see me put a knife right into your heart. That's why that tent wasn't but half filled till you stepped inside the outline. You can see it in the way they squint their eyes, trying to send mind messages so I'll screw up."

"Then look into my eyes, listen for my mind messages," I said, pulling Ricky close to me.

And that's what he'd done. Before each throw his eyes met mine and I thought hard as I could, willing his knife to the right place.

Most of the time, and always on the first night in a new town, I'd be seated in the stands. Ricky would start off throwing at the outline and soon enough someone in the bleachers would complain or demand a refund. Then I'd volunteer and the townies would whoop and clap. When we did it that way they always left more satisfied, thinking they'd gotten more than they'd paid for.

I'd always sit in the same place in the bleachers, end of the third row, because Ricky liked things done the same way every time. He had other rituals as well. He'd get dressed thirty minutes before the show, then take each knife from the carrying case and rub it with a piece of black velvet. He'd turn on his tape player and lie on the bed with his eyes closed.

He played the same song each time, "Don't Fear the Reefer," which seemed a strange kind of choice since Ricky didn't drink, much less smoke marijuana. As soon as the song ended he got up and went straight to the tent.

Everything had gone well the first five months. Then one night as we lay in the sawdust, Ricky said he loved me.

"I've known that a long time, baby," I said, brushing the sawdust from his hair. "But it's nice to hear you say it."

"I've known it a long time too," Ricky said, his voice low and serious. "I just didn't want to admit it, not so much to you but to myself."

I lay my head against his chest.

"Why not?"

"Because love for me is all or nothing. I don't know how to hold anything back," Ricky said. "You'd think that car wreck would have taught me different but it didn't."

"That's who you are, Ricky. That's the kind of people we are."

"And you're glad of that?" Ricky asked.

"I haven't always been," I said. "But I am now. I want you to be glad too, Ricky."

After that night Ricky no longer looked in my eyes when he threw. He'd look above me, below me, anywhere but at me. His aim suffered, most of the time wider and wider, sometimes not even hitting the plywood.

"Hell, boy," a townie in Shelby, North Carolina, had said. "My blind granny could get closer than that."

But sometimes he had gotten too close, the knife so near the handle would brush my skin as it wavered. And now he had drawn blood.

"WHAT YOU WAITING for?" a townie wearing a cowboy hat shouted at Ricky.

"It's just getting interesting," a bald-headed man on the front row added.

"Show's over," I said, my index finger feeling the depth of the cut. "You got more than your money's worth."

"But he only thrown one knife."

"That's right," I said, "and if he'd thrown it eight inches farther to the right, I'd be a dead woman."

I stepped away from the plywood as the bleachers emptied.

"Here," I said, handing Ricky his knife. "I'm going back to the trailer and sew up this blouse. When you get your knives packed, you come on home. We need to talk this thing out."

I stepped out of the tent and walked down the midway, everything looking the same to me as it would for someone who lived in a regular home in a regular neighborhood, for though we were two states away from where we'd been last weekend, nothing had changed. The tents remained in the same order, from the Snake Man's at the start of the midway to the Human Skeleton's down at the end. The air smelled of corn dogs and cotton candy and the same rides circled and plunged while the same neon lights rainbowed the night.

The Human Skeleton stood outside his tent sipping a Diet Coke.

"Damn, Ellie," he said. "Looks like you earned your money tonight. If Ricky keeps whittling off your flesh you might end up working with me."

"I reckon so," I said and walked behind the tent and up the steps of me and Ricky's camper.

Ricky came in a few minutes later, quiet and tense, the way he'd been the last few days.

"So what is it?" I asked, and if he'd been any other man I'd known he'd have hemmed and hawed an hour before answering that question. But that wasn't the way we were with each other.

"I'm afraid I'll lose you," he said. "Seems that's what happened to anyone I've ever cared about. You might get tired of this life before long and start looking for a man who can give you a home you can turn around in without bumping into the other person, a yard with grass instead of sawdust. You may decide you want kids, and if you do you'll not want them living this kind of life."

I could have said the easy things, maybe the true things—that I'd always want to be with the carnival and would always be happy living in a camper trailer. Or said the thing I most believed, which was that I'd always be with him, and if I did have children I'd want to have them with him, because I'd never find another man who could give me the kind of nothing-held-back love he'd given me. But I didn't, because *always* is a tricky word, especially concerning matters of the heart.

"I don't feel that way now," I said. "But I'm twenty-four, Ricky. How can I know for sure what I'll want?"

"I don't want to ever lose you," Ricky said.

I stepped over to him, lay my hand on his face.

"I don't want to lose you either, baby," I said.

Ricky closed his eyes.

"Now when I throw I get afraid. I think about what could happen if . . . I could lose you that way too."

"That's how it is, Ricky," I said, "at least in the kind of relationship me and you have. Maybe it's best when nothing's held back, nothing's taken for granted."

And when I said that I thought about nights after we'd finish the performance, the knives that had whizzed inches from my flesh still stuck in the plywood. The last townie would barely be out of the tent and Ricky and me would be tearing the clothes off each other like they were on fire. We'd make love right there in the sawdust, unable to wait the two minutes it would take to get to the camper. Because we'd taken each other to a place few people go together, a place where your faith in each other is a matter of life and death—him believing I wouldn't move an inch, me believing his aim would be true. Those moments I felt more alive than any time in my life, and I could tell Ricky felt the same way. We'd lay there covered with sweat and sawdust, our hearts pressed against each other's, as close as two human beings can ever be.

"I want you to wear this," Ricky said, and pulled from under the bed what looked like a cross between a corset and a knight's armor. "It'll fit under your clothes. Nobody will know the difference."

I felt the weight of the thing, lighter than you'd expect.

Nobody but you and me, I thought.

"I'm tired," Ricky said. He pulled off his boots and clothes and lay down in the bed, his face turned to the wall.

I sat in the chair and stared at Ricky's back, the back my hands moved across nights our bodies merged into what seemed the sweet everlasting. I could hear the music and loudspeakers and shrieks as the townies got flung around the sky, but everything outside that camper seemed miles away. I was deep inside myself, thinking things out.

I laid the body armor beside the door and undressed. I lay down beside Ricky, my breasts touching his back, my arm on his side, my hand spread across his stomach. I knew he was still awake. I moved my hand higher, feeling the smooth skin, the hair on his chest.

"Don't," he said, removing my hand.

I lay there listening to the noises, knowing neither of us would sleep much that night. I got up after a while and went to the pay phone out by the front gate.

Momma answered on the fourth ring, still half asleep.

"What's wrong, Ellie?" she said, because after midnight she knew well as me no one calls with good news.

"It's complicated."

"Then I reckon there's a man involved," Momma said. "Are you and Ricky having problems?"

"Yes, but not what you'd think."

"So it's not money, drinking, or snoring."

"No, ma'am."

"Well, if it's sex you best read *Cosmopolitan*. All I know is what it's like for me and your daddy, and I got the feeling you'd rather not know the details."

"It's not that, either. Ricky says he's afraid he loves me too much."

"Well," Momma said, "all I can say is there's many a woman who would be happy to have that kind of problem."

Right then I knew there was no way to explain it to Momma. There was one person who could help me work this out and he was back at the camper.

"Yes, Momma," I finally said. "I guess you're right. I'm sorry I woke you."

I walked back to the trailer and lay next to Ricky. His breath was deep and regular, and I knew he'd finally managed to fall asleep. I thought how it had been with Robert and how one morning I'd woke up and felt to be in bed with a stranger. I thought about the family photos, how I was always on the edge, almost out of the picture—even in the five-by-seven black-and-whites somehow apart from the rest of the family. I thought about how the last eight months I'd found something that finally felt like home. Because home for me wasn't so much a place but a feeling you were where you should be, and at the center of that feeling was Ricky. I finally went to sleep. I dreamed I stood in front of the plywood. Ricky was down at the far end of the tent, a bow in his hands. It was not knives that crossed the space between us. It was arrows.

WE SLEPT TILL noon the next day, and in the hours before the show we had little to say to each other. Ricky and me had always been good at talking to one another, but it was like we'd taken ourselves to a place where we needed a new language, a language we hadn't yet learned to speak.

At six-thirty Ricky lay down on the bed. "Don't Fear the Reefer" blasted through the speakers. I listened to the words careful, hoping they might say something Ricky's words couldn't say. And they did, because I suddenly realized I'd been hearing the song wrong. The singer was saying "Don't fear the reaper," not "Don't fear the reefer."

Ricky left the camper before I did. I changed into my blouse and skirt but left the body armor by the door. The Human Skeleton was leaving his camper at the same time I was, so we walked to the midway together.

"We got a change in the weather coming," he said. "I can feel it in my bones."

I walked into the tent and saw the bleachers were already full. Ricky stood near the entrance, his knife case open. I pressed my back against the plywood. When Ricky picked up his first knife and turned to face me, I raised my hands and unbuttoned my blouse until the V between my breasts showed. The townies cheered and clapped but that meant nothing to me. My eyes and

Ricky's met as the world narrowed to the twenty feet from him to me. He raised the knife to his ear as if the blade might whisper something to him. Then his arm came forward and the knife flashed out of his hand, closing the distance between us.

❖

The Projectionist's Wife

One warm December morning forty years ago I stood in a grove of oak trees, the blood on my face confirming what I already knew. At my feet lay what the old deer slayers called a hart—a big male with antlers sprouting like coral from its forehead. My right hand gripped a Browning 30-30, the rifle I'd raised earlier that morning to defend Mrs. Merwin, the projectionist's wife, a woman who came from a place that did not exist.

"Drink up," my uncle had said earlier that morning as he handed me a cup of coffee. "You can't be snoozing when a deer comes your way."

I nodded, too sleep-dazed to speak. The grandfather clock

chimed five o'clock as I sipped the black coffee, ate the gravy and cathead biscuits my uncle made as I dressed. We spoke in whispers, because my mother and aunt still slept in the back rooms. My father had died when I was eight, leaving behind a son and a twenty-nine-year-old widow, who now spent what remained of her early adulthood working inside the town's paper plant. My uncle, besides giving my mother and me a place to live, served as a surrogate father. He taught me how to use a saw and ax, catch and clean a trout, and hunt—first tin cans scattered on a hillside, then squirrels and rabbits, finally, at age twelve, deer.

Often my first cousin Jeff or my uncle's neighbor Luke Callahan hunted with us. I liked Jeff but did not care much for Mr. Callahan, a red-nosed, scarecrow-thin man who drank too much and told jokes I did not understand. Unlike Jeff, I hadn't been blooded yet, my only shot a flash of antler behind trees. I'd watched enviously the previous November as my uncle and Mr. Callahan dipped their hands in the warm blood, reddened Jeff's face as if the blood was war paint.

"You ain't a man till you get blooded, boy," Mr. Callahan had said, looking at me as he tasted the deer blood on his fingers. "I killed my first deer when I was ten."

"All Russell needs is a decent shot," my uncle said. "He's shot targets all summer so he wouldn't get rusty. He's been hitting them too. His time will come, Luke, and he'll be ready."

And I was ready to be a man. I saw my body's readiness in the stubble on my chin, the way I'd sprouted four inches over the summer. I felt a readiness inside me as well, not as I waited in that deer stand but in the darkness of the Enlo Cinema.

The theater Mr. and Mrs. Merwin ran was the one exotic place in a town I always remember in shades of gray, in large part because of Carolina Paper Company, whose twin smokestacks sooted the whole valley. Most of Enlo's adults worked inside that mill. They all seemed to wear an ashy pallor, as if it were papier-mâché instead of flesh wrapped around their bones. But it was more than the paper mill, the grown-ups it swallowed for eight hours each day, or even the highland weather when so many days passed in a monotone of fog and drizzle. It was the surrounding mountains themselves, the way they cast huge daggers of shadow over the valley, blocked any distant gaze as we moved beneath in the gloaming like cave fish.

And this was why stepping into that theater lobby was like stepping into a radiant dream—the multihued coming-attraction posters, shelves of bright-wrapped candy, the popcorn machine's yellow lambency. Mrs. Merwin was a part of that brightness. She dressed bright as a parrot from head to toe, the cloth tight against her skin, mouth rimmed scarlet with lipstick, a woman literally from nowhere who'd suddenly appeared in Enlo's midst. It was she who allowed me entrance, sitting in the ticket booth like a fortune-teller, exchanging the coins my mother had reluctantly given me for two hours' respite from a dreariness that seeped through my skin to my very bones.

Mrs. Merwin was the only person in town I could imagine describing as glamorous, not only how she dressed but how she smelled, her perfume ordered directly from Europe, Mr. Lusk the postmaster said. She spoke a different English as well, faster, sounding out her *g* and *d* endings. Even her first name was glamorous, a consonant-thick montage no one in Enlo but her husband could pronounce.

Mrs. Merwin told those who asked that she had been born in a country that no longer existed. Her parents were descended from nobility, but they had lost everything in the war, even their country. Whether what she said was true no one really knew, except perhaps Mr. Merwin, who'd brought her back from Europe as his war bride, but he was a gruff man who said little even to his kinsmen, a man who had no children of his own and little use for those who entered his theater.

Mr. Merwin was a projectionist, a man most comfortable in the hunched darkness of his profession. When the last ticket was sold, he left his wife to attend the concession stand, disappearing through the curtain next to the bathrooms and up the winding metal stairs. There was no balcony, so he sat alone up there, a wizard who brought forth nightly illusions with a weave of his hands as he threaded film through the projector and the movie sputtered to life. But Mr. Merwin seemed to cast a spell on everyone except himself. Perhaps as the source of that mirage, he knew too well that the bright worlds holding his audience transfixed were mere celluloid, easily bottled up in the gray canisters he exchanged in Asheville every Thursday morning. Mr. Merwin appeared immune to the spell his wife cast as well, as terse with her as he was to any child.

"I don't know why she stays with that old grump," my aunt said one Sunday. She, my mother, and my uncle lingered at the dinner table as I oiled the Browning in the front room and pretended not to listen. "He should have known better than marry a woman that much younger. I wouldn't be surprised if she just up and left him."

"Where would she go?" my uncle asked. "Her country doesn't exist anymore."

"So she says," my mother said. "I have my doubts about that, about a lot of things she's claimed. We know what that war did to Arthur Merwin. He's got scars and a Purple Heart to prove it. Besides, he gives her enough money to buy those fancy clothes and French perfume."

"That could be her money," my aunt said, "and probably is. I've never known a Merwin that was more than one paycheck from the poorhouse."

"Well, all I know," said my mother with finality, "is that a woman who dresses like that is looking for trouble, and sooner or later she'll find it. As a matter of fact, I hear she's been finding it for a while now. I suspicion Arthur knows what's going on too."

At the time it was easy to believe my aunt's and uncle's sympathies were more admirable than my mother's. Those nights as I sat in the darkened theater I sometimes glanced back at the beam of light aimed at the screen. I wondered if Mr. Merwin was watching not the movie but the audience, and that made me feel uneasy. But I could not be sure what he was doing up there, since the light was too bright to look at for more than a moment.

What I do know is that when I was fourteen, his wife was as beautiful as any of the screen goddesses I watched in his theater. On Friday or Saturday nights I sat a few rows behind the girls in my ninth-grade class, girls whose bodies grew more curved and mysterious daily. I anointed myself with my dead father's Aqua Velva and it wafted over the rows between us like a promise that I too was growing up. What they were becoming, Mrs. Merwin, with her hourglass figure and low, throaty voice, already was.

I waited until the MGM lion roared and IN CINEMASCOPE appeared in five-foot-high letters. Only then did I leave my seat, make my way blindly up the inclining carpet toward the red-glowing exit sign. The lobby was empty now, just me and Mrs. Merwin.

"What will you have, Russell?" she'd ask as I inhaled an odor like a field of flowers, and it was as if the smell rose like vapors into my brain and made me groggy, for inevitably I'd forget what I'd planned to order. Once I finally stammered out a few words, Mrs. Merwin would hand me my drink and whatever I'd chosen to eat. As she leaned forward to place the money in the metal box, I could see the globes of her breasts, the dark V between them. Then I'd sit back down in the dark, dazed by the wide worlds projected on the screen, by the girls who sat with me in the dark, but most of all by Mrs. Merwin.

IT WAS A late December Thursday when I discovered Mrs. Merwin was also part of the gray valley outside the theater. I was out of school for Christmas, and my uncle Roy, Luke Callahan, and I were hunting. The older men had given me the stand closest to the dirt road, only yards from the dead end that marked the boundary between my uncle's land and state game lands.

"Don't shoot toward the road," my uncle reminded me. "We'll be back at eleven. If it starts raining we'll meet you at the house."

"Don't let the haints get you, boy." Luke Callahan smirked, and they disappeared into the deeper woods, only the sound of their footsteps crushing the leaves, then nothing.

The sun was nowhere to be seen. Fog swirled around the deer stand like a current, and the wood planks swayed and creaked as if I were on a raft. I waited for the sound of deer hooves, trying not to think about the old woman who'd lost her way in these woods years ago. She'd been found by my grandfather, days dead, her back against a tree trunk as if waiting for him. Some people claimed she still walked these woods.

The curtain of fog did not lift as I crouched in the stand, the rifle cradled in my lap. Only the closest trees were visible, and the woods remained silent, no squirrels rustling the leaves, no crow cawing from a treetop. I checked my watch. The hands had moved so little I raised my wrist to my ear. Everything—trees, sound, time—seemed lost in the fog.

Then I heard the crackling of leaves, close, maybe thirty yards away, and coming closer, and despite what my uncle had told me I raised my rifle toward the road, peered into the scope, my thumb on the safety, index finger on the trigger. I heard voices, one voice I knew—then silence. They had stopped walking, stopped talking. I waited, the rifle still pressed against my shoulder, still aimed.

"No, not here," Mrs. Merwin said. "It's too close to the road." She stepped out of the fog, and into the crosshairs of my rifle, one strap of her dress pulled off her shoulder, lipstick smeared on her face. A man I did not know followed her, a half-empty whiskey bottle in his hand.

"Yeah, here," the man said, grabbing her arm with his free hand, snatching the quilts from her and dropping them on the ground.

"No," Mrs. Merwin said. "Please, Lance, not here."

He yanked the dress strap lower with his free hand, a pale breast fully exposed now.

"No," she said and pushed him away.

The man stepped closer and slapped her, the sound sharp as a rifle shot. The left side of Mrs. Merwin's face flushed scarlet. I saw the imprint of his hand and my thumb released the safety.

"Leave her alone," I said, the gun trembling in my hands.

They did not see me at first, and it must have seemed the voice of God speaking from above. Mrs. Merwin covered her bare breast with one hand, pulled the strap up with the other. The man stood absolutely still, his hand open as if to slap anyone else who came near.

Then they found me, the man seeing the rifle, Mrs. Merwin seeing my face, or so it seemed, for the man's first words were "Put that rifle down, boy." Mrs. Merwin said, "Hello, Russell," as if I'd just stepped up to her ticket booth. I did not lower the rifle. I kept it pointed at them, the barrel wavering like a compass needle.

"Put that rifle down, boy," the man repeated.

"You hit her again I'll shoot you," I said.

"It's okay, Russell," Mrs. Merwin said. "He didn't hurt me. He's my friend."

I thumbed the safety back on, lowered the rifle.

"Come down here," the man said, but I wasn't coming down.

"Russell," Mrs. Merwin said. "This is not what it seems." But it was exactly what it seemed, and we all knew it. No one said anything else. No one moved. We were like actors waiting for a cue that never came.

"We're leaving now, Russell," Mrs. Merwin finally said, picking up the quilts. "I hope you won't say anything about this. People might not understand."

The man started to say something, something threatening from his tone, but Mrs. Merwin hushed him.

"Please, Russell," she said. "Don't say anything."

"Okay," I said.

She turned then, walked back toward the road, the man following her. They disappeared into the fog like apparitions.

ENLO IS A small town, and though I did not go to the theater in the following weeks, I eventually saw Mrs. Merwin. It was a cold afternoon in February, and my uncle had dropped me off to pick up a prescription while he ran some other errands. As I entered the drugstore I saw Mrs. Merwin across the street. She was dressed in a brown overcoat, her broom swaying back and forth as she swept the sidewalk in front of the theater. She was waiting for me when I stepped back outside.

"I've been wanting to talk to you," she said.

I didn't want to meet her eyes, so I looked past her to where the paper mill's smokestacks smoldered like snuffed-out birthday candles.

"I want to thank you," she said, "for not telling. I made a mistake. That man that was with me, I'm never going to see him again. I wanted you to know that, Russell."

I nodded, still not looking at her. I shoved my hands in my

pockets and waited for her to finish whatever it was she felt compelled to tell me.

"What you did, trying to protect me from him, that took courage. What I'm saying is, in all this you've been very grown-up." She smiled. "You've been my knight in shining armor."

She turned then, clasping the lapels of her overcoat, and walked back across the street. I stood on the sidewalk in front of the drugstore, hands in my pockets, watching her disappear into the theater.

I knew she was right about my being a man. I had killed my deer that same morning, less than an hour after I'd seen her and her lover in the woods. I heard leaves crunched softly and slow, deliberate footsteps moving toward me. I thought it might be Mrs. Merwin's lover. I aimed the rifle into the gray swirl for the second time that morning, not knowing if I could pull the trigger. Then the deer stepped into the crosshairs of my scope. I took a deep breath, held it, aimed for the shoulder, and squeezed.

"A perfect shot," my uncle said later as he and Mr. Callahan kneeled beside the deer, rubbing their hands in the blood that pooled on the flank.

"You're a man now," Mr. Callahan said, reeking of whiskey as he and my uncle dabbed my face, a drop dribbling onto my lips. The blood tasted like metal.

THE FOLLOWING SPRING Mrs. Merwin left her husband and Enlo. Most people assume she went back to Europe, looking for a place that no longer existed. I remember her at odd moments—when I smell a certain perfume, see an attractive woman dressed in a colorful outfit—and the past comes into focus, in such vividness it is almost tactile. I also think of her husband, years dead now. At age fifty-four I see him as I could not at fourteen, not so much an ill-humored wizard as a weary clockmaker god threading the stuff of dreams through the projector's metal maze, then onto the second reel so he might watch in impotent solitude as his work slowly unraveled before him.

❖

Deep Gap

After the second time his hardware store had been robbed, both times at night, Marshall Vaughn bought a pistol. He kept it under the counter, but unlike his younger brother, Keith, a highway patrolman, Marshall was sixty before he needed to point the pistol at another human being, and it wasn't in his store but in an apartment 150 miles away.

He had not killed the men, but he knew he could have and would have if they'd not left when he told them to. At the time, it was as if some part of himself left his body, the way people claimed in near-death experiences. He'd seen not only his son and the two black men but himself as well, as though he were watching the whole event from behind a one-way mirror. Later Marshall wondered if somehow his soul had indeed left his body the moment he'd stepped inside that apartment.

What he'd found in there was worse than he had imagined, and what he'd imagined had scared him enough to bring the pistol. The door was unlocked, and inside all the shades were down and the only light came from a TV. The room reeked of unwashed flesh, spoiled food left on plates and in boxes, and whatever had filled the pipes strewn on the floor like toys after a child's tantrum.

Brad did not turn his face from the TV screen when Marshall spoke his son's name. Only the black men looked up.

"What the hell do you want?" one of the men demanded.

"He's going home with me," Marshall said.

There had been other words after that, and when things got to a point where words were useless, Marshall brought out the gun. The men left, and quick as Marshall loaded up Brad's possessions in the Camry, he and Brad left also and drove west toward Deep Gap.

"Don't you even care that you're killing yourself?" Marshall asked, but his son did not reply. Instead, Brad leaned his head against the passenger-seat window and closed his eyes. As they drove out of the city Marshall remembered weekend fishing trips to Price Lake. They would leave at dawn, Brad sleeping all the way, but soon as Marshall parked the car Brad's eyes would spring open and the boy would gather his rod and tackle box. They'd fish two hours and return home in time to open the hardware store at nine or, if it was Sunday, to get dressed for church. That was before Linda had come to find the role of mother and wife, in her words, "too confining." After she left, there never seemed to be time for fishing trips.

MARSHALL WENT BACK to Brad's apartment the next weekend, and he drove his pickup instead of the Camry. He cleaned up the place as best he could, filling the back of the truck with bulging trash bags. He settled up with the apartment complex manager. While still in the city limits he stopped at a convenience store and threw the trash bags in a Dumpster. He wanted to carry as little of Charlotte back to Deep Gap as possible.

Now, six months later—after Brad's two months in a drug rehab center, after two more months with a counselor in Lenoir—two young men came into the hardware store and Marshall soon realized nothing but the locale and the skin color of the drug dealers had changed.

"What can I do for you?" Marshall asked when the one whose eyes were not hidden by a Carolina Panthers ball cap stepped closer. The man pulled a check out of his jeans pocket and laid it on the counter. Marshall read the name on the check and the amount and then looked back at the man who stood before him. He wore a black T-shirt that provided a sharp contrast to the pale, unlined skin, the long, blond hair and wispy mustache. Marshall guessed him to be in his mid-twenties.

"It bounced," the man said. The voice did not sound native, and Marshall guessed he was probably a college student who'd stayed in Boone after graduating or flunking out. The man nodded at the check. "We want our money."

The other young man stepped closer and Marshall saw enough of a face beneath the cap's bill to recognize Larry Crawford's youngest son, Jared. He and Larry had grown up together back when Boone was a one-stoplight town. They'd attended the same schools and the same church, and now Larry ran a service station in Boone just two blocks from Vaughn Hardware.

"We didn't want to go to the bank about this check, Mr. Vaughn," Jared said, his eyes hidden by the cap. "We figured we ought to come to you first."

"I've got a feeling your father wouldn't be too proud of you right now," Marshall said.

The other blond-haired man spoke.

"This doesn't concern his father. It's about getting what's owed us."

Marshall paid them, and though it was only four-thirty he put the Closed sign on the front door. As he drove down Main Street he passed Blue Ridge Texaco. Larry Crawford cleaned the windshield of a car parked in front of the full-service island. Unlike Marshall, Larry hadn't had the chance to buy out a sibling and own a family business. "Must be nice to have something like that handed to you," Larry had said to him once. "All my old man gave me was some good whippings and a final hospital bill to pay off." Marshall had been surprised at the bitterness in Larry's voice. Marshall wondered if it was possible some part of Larry might be pleased that a Vaughn owed a Crawford money, even if that money was for drugs.

There were eight stoplights in Boone now. Traffic moved in congested lurches from one light to the next. Ten minutes passed before Marshall got to the turnoff that took him toward Deep

Gap, toward the trailer he'd rented for Brad three months ago. The trailer sat on land three miles from Marshall's house, the house Brad had grown up in. Close to home but far enough away, as the counselor had suggested, that Brad felt some independence. Which was also the reason for the checking account, another of the counselor's suggestions.

ONCE HE WAS clear of the Boone city limit sign, Marshall turned on the radio. An archaeologist discussed recent evidence that the Americas had been inhabited by humans much earlier than previously thought, and not only by people of Asian origin but also by Africans and Europeans. These earlier cultures had their own distinct ways of making tools, their own burial customs and languages. Then they had simply disappeared. No one knew if they'd died out because of famine or disease or had been annihilated or assimilated by other tribes.

The Camry Marshall had given Brad so he could drive to work and to counseling was parked by the trailer. Marshall didn't knock before he entered. Brad lay sprawled out on the couch, watching cartoon characters flash across the TV screen. The flesh around his eyes was puffy. Brad wore only a pair of ragged boxer shorts, though the window air-conditioning unit cooled the room enough that condensation formed on the windows. The trailer reeked of drugs. It was like formaldehyde to Marshall, an odor not forgotten once smelled.

"Why aren't you at work?" he asked.

Brad did not look away from the cartoon.

"Didn't feel up to it."

"Jarvis Greene did me a personal favor hiring you," Marshall said. "The least you can do is show up for work."

Marshall took the check from his pocket and held it out to his son.

"I paid it, but I swear to God I won't the next time."

"So," Brad said. "I never asked you to pay it. I never asked for that job either."

Marshall had never struck his son, never even spanked him, but a part of him wanted to strike him now, this moment, and not stop until he drew blood, maybe not stop even then. Like six months earlier in Charlotte, it was as though a door stood before him that, once opened, he'd never be able to close. Marshall made himself speak, afraid to let the silence intensify what he felt.

"I'm the only person on this earth that gives a damn about you. Your drug dealers don't. You sure don't."

Marshall did not mention Brad's mother. That was understood, had been for a decade. Still, a part of Marshall wanted to mention her, wanted to say, whether it was true or not, that much of what had gone wrong in Brad's life could be traced back to her desertion.

"That counselor is right about one thing, Son. If you don't think your life's worth something, then sooner or later no one else will."

Marshall paused at the door.

"Don't miss work again. Jarvis Greene's not going to put up with that kind of sorry behavior, and I wouldn't expect him to."

As he drove back to the store, Marshall wondered if he'd made Brad go to college at Appalachian instead of UNC, Charlotte, or if Linda had left a few years later, his son's life might have been different. Once Linda was gone, should he have closed the hardware store at four instead of six. When Brad had grown more remote, should he have tried harder to talk to him, kept better tabs on him during high school.

Marshall wanted to believe that there was no single moment in Brad's life when it all began to go wrong—a moment that might have been avoided. He wished he could believe that whatever had so flawed his son was inevitable, no different than a child born with cerebral palsy or a malfunctioning heart.

WHEN HE GOT back to Boone, Marshall thought about phoning Keith at the highway patrol office, then decided to walk down to Blue Ridge Texaco instead. Larry Crawford was in the garage changing the oil on a Mercedes with Florida plates, his hands and forearms and brow blackened by oil and grease. Larry tightened the drain plug and stepped out from under the car.

"What you need, Marshall?" he asked as he wiped his hands on a rag.

"If you got a minute I'd like to talk to you about our boys."

"I got a minute," Larry said.

Marshall told him about the visit that morning in the hardware store, about the check and what that check was for.

Larry stuffed the rag in his back pocket.

"Jared's twenty-five years old," Larry said. "Like your son he's a man and way past the time for me to tell him what he can and can't do."

"So this doesn't bother you?" Marshall asked.

"I didn't say that," Larry said.

"You're telling me it's something you'd have considered do-ing when we were his age?" Marshall asked. "I know you better than that."

"You know me, do you?" Larry said. He wiped sweat off his forehead with the back of his hand, lengthening the black smudge on his brow. "Well, I'll tell you something. I don't blame Jared. I'm fifty-eight years old, and I spend my day changing oil and pumping gas for college students and tourists so my boss can af-ford a second home at Myrtle Beach. And what have I got? I'm near deaf and my back and knees hurt all the time. I wouldn't want Jared to live as sorry a life as this."

"Even if it means going to jail if he gets caught?" Marshall asked.

"There's all different kinds of jails."

"I can tell Keith about what Jared is doing," Marshall said, "and you can bet he'll put an end to it. I almost did but came to see you instead."

A Jeep pulled up to the full-service island.

"You'll do what you're going to do," Larry said. "Just make sure you ain't blaming the wrong person for your boy's problem."

Larry took out the rag and wiped his hands again.

"I got work to do," he said and walked toward the Jeep.

THAT NIGHT MARSHALL had trouble sleeping. He woke at first light and could not fall back asleep. He dressed and made coffee, then went out to sit on the front porch. He owned twelve acres but each year his land seemed less a homestead than a shrinking island. Developers had bought up most of the surrounding farms and turned them into subdivisions and gated communities. There had been a time he knew every man, woman, and child in Deep Gap on a first-name basis. A time he could see only one other house from his front porch. Now he could see two dozen, their yards and driveways replacing what were once pastures and fields.

"Cultures disappear, are replaced by other cultures, and that's as it should be," the archaeologist on the radio had said. Marshall had no problem understanding the disappearing part. As a child, he'd found arrowheads and pottery shards in his neighbors' fields, occasionally even in the vegetable garden his father tilled behind the house. They surfaced from the ground like afterthoughts, something briefly remembered before being forgotten again.

And not so different from the men who'd once come into the hardware store on Saturdays. Men who wore dirt-crusted brogans and Red Camel overalls and who after their sales were rung up lingered awhile to talk, sometimes about hunting and fishing, sometimes religion and politics, inevitably, the weather.

Only a few such men were left in the county now, all old. They'd been replaced by college professors and wealthy retirees, people who liked the "quaintness" of Marshall's store—the smell of linseed oil on the oak floors, the potbellied stove and ceiling fan. That was why they shopped at Vaughn Hardware instead of True Value or Kmart. Marshall knew they found him and his mountain accent quaint as well, were always surprised and a little disappointed when they came in and heard NPR on the radio, or found out he had a degree in agriculture from N.C. State.

"You're a dying breed," a retiree from Ohio had told him last month. "When that Wal-Mart comes next year they'll cut your business in half."

At a few minutes after eight, just as Marshall prepared to leave for Boone, the phone rang.

"I had to fire Brad," Jarvis Greene said. "You know how it is with a construction crew. You let one man lay out and pretty soon the whole crew figures they can get away with it as well."

"I know," Marshall said. "You gave him a chance. That's all I expected and I appreciate your doing that."

Marshall put down the receiver. For a few moments he debated calling either the counselor in Lenoir or his brother at the highway patrol office. But he didn't. As he drove to the hardware store, Marshall remembered the first months after Linda had left, how Brad, though twelve at the time, had insisted on sleeping with him every night. Once the boy had waked him at three in the morning. "You won't ever leave me?" he'd asked, and Marshall had held him close and promised he never would. At that moment Marshall knew Brad would have made the same promise to him had he asked. But not now, Marshall thought, not now.

TWO WEEKS PASSED before Jared Crawford showed up at the hardware store, another worthless check in his hand. He came in alone.

"I'm not giving you anymore money," Marshall said.

"Somebody's got to pay us," Jared said, refusing to meet Marshall's eyes. "Me and John got people to pay too."

"Then why did you take a check you knew was worthless, Jared?" Marshall asked.

"We got to be paid," Jared said, his cheeks reddening, still not meeting Marshall's eyes.

At least he's got some sense of shame about this, Marshall thought.

"You take that up with Brad," he said. "That's between you and him."

"We've already did that," Jared said. "He said he didn't have any money."

"Where is your buddy?" Marshall asked.

"He wouldn't come, didn't want me to come here either. He wants to go over to Brad's trailer and take Brad's TV and CD player. If that don't make us square he figures to take the rest out of Brad's hide."

Jared finally looked at him.

"He's going to do that this afternoon, Mr. Vaughn, if you don't pay. That's why I came."

"I'm not going to pay," Marshall said. "I told you that once already. How about leaving now. Some folks actually still work for a living."

Only a few customers came in during the afternoon, so Marshall spent much of the time unloading boxes in the back room. There had been changes in the front part of the store—fluorescent lights, electric heat, shelves stocked with bird and grass seed instead of tobacco and corn seed, lawn mowers and rakes filling corners instead of hoes and plows.

But the back room was the same as half a century ago when Marshall first began helping his father and grandfather run the store on weekends. A single dusty forty-watt bulb hung from the ceiling. Tin signs advertising DeKalb corn seed and Aladdin lamps were nailed on unpainted wall planks. The smell of sweet feed lingered, as did the smell of the Prince Albert pipe tobacco his grandfather and father had smoked. As Marshall opened the first box, he looked around and realized the world he understood had been reduced to this one room.

Marshall waited until four-thirty before he turned the sign on the door. He lifted the gun from under the counter and took it with him.

Once he got to Deep Gap he turned right at the intersection, opposite the road that led to Brad's trailer. Marshall drove slowly past where his elementary school had been, past the land his grand-parents had once owned. He drove up back roads he hadn't been on in years. He looked through the present into the past, bringing back farmhouses and barns and pastures and woods.

He did not drive to Brad's trailer until the dashboard clock said six. The only car parked out front was the Camry. The TV and radio were gone and an open window gaped where the air-conditioning unit had been. Brad lay on the bed in the back room. One eye was swollen completely shut, and a cut below the eye would need stitches. When Marshall asked if anything was bro-ken, Brad pointed to his ribs. Marshall pressed the flat of his hand against his son's left side and the boy's face tightened.

Marshall had learned in Charlotte he could take another man's life. Now he believed he could take his own. He stepped back from his son and showed the pistol, past some point he could not give a name to.

"If you want me to end this right now I'll do it," Marshall said, "but it's got to be both of us. I'll even go first if that's what you want."

Brad started to speak, but Marshall stopped him.

"Don't answer quick. Think about it first and think about it hard."

Marshall laid the gun on the bedside table, then walked into the front room. He stared through the open window where the air conditioner had been. Osborne Mountain rose in the distance, above it a blue sky so deep it seemed not so much a color as a clearness beyond distance and time. Marshall knew there were houses on that mountain but distance and summer foliage hid them. Eight or ten thousand years ago a man would have seen nothing more than this, a leaf-greened mountain and a blue sky.

When he went back the gun was on the table.

"So you want me to go first?" Marshall asked.

"No, I don't want that, for you or me," Brad said. "I want to get better."

Marshall felt more resignation than relief when he heard his son's words. There would be no quick fixes for either of them. It might take weeks or months or even years before either one of them knew if Brad could live the truth of what he now claimed. But that was what he would do, try to save his son, because there was nothing else left to save.

"Can you walk?" Marshall asked, and Brad shook his head.

Marshall lifted his son from the bed. Though Brad was thirty pounds lighter than Marshall, it still wasn't easy. Just getting him off the bed and into his arms took several tries, and he nearly tripped going down the trailer's cement steps. By the time Brad lay on the Camry's backseat Marshall gasped for breath.

Brad had not moaned or whimpered though Marshall knew the jostling must have been excruciating. As he drove toward the hospital Marshall remembered another moment years earlier when he'd made a similar trip.

Brad was playing in the creek below the house and had come too close to a hornets' nest. Marshall was on the front porch reading the paper when the boy came running toward him, hornets swirling around his terrified face like a malevolent halo.

Marshall had run to meet him, swatting the hornets with the paper, picking them off the boy's skin and hair. He'd been stung several times himself, but Brad had been stung a dozen times, all on the face and neck. Linda hadn't been home, so Marshall had laid Brad in the backseat of the Plymouth station wagon.

"It's going to be all right," he'd reassured his son that morning twenty years earlier. He said those same words now, willing himself and Brad to believe them as they rode together toward a place where the injured came to be healed.

❖

Pemberton's Bride

I

When Pemberton returned to the North Carolina mountains after four months in Boston settling his father's estate, among those waiting on the train platform was a woman pregnant with Pemberton's child. She was accompanied by her father, a man named Harmon who carried beneath his shabby frock coat a bowie knife sharpened with great attentiveness earlier that morning so it would plunge as deep as possible into Pemberton's heart.

The conductor shouted "Waynesville" as the train came to a shuddering halt. Pemberton looked out the window and saw his partners on the platform, both dressed in suits to meet his bride of three days, an unexpected bonus from his time in Boston. Buchanan, ever the dandy, had waxed his mustache and oiled his hair. Peabody wore a fedora, as he often did to protect his bald head from the sun. Pemberton took out his gold pocket watch and saw the train was on time to the exact minute. He turned to his bride.

"Not the best place for a honeymoon."

"It will suit us well enough," Serena said, leaning into his shoulder. As she did so, he smelled the bright aroma of Ivory soap and remembered tasting that brightness on her skin earlier that morning. A porter came up the aisle, whistling a song Pemberton did not recognize. His gaze returned to the window.

Next to the ticket booth Harmon and his daughter waited, Harmon slouched against the chestnut wall. It struck Pemberton that males in these mountains never stood upright but rather slouched or leaned into some tree or wall whenever possible. If none were available they squatted, buttocks against the backs of their heels. The daughter sat on the bench, her posture upright to better reveal her condition. Pemberton could not recall her first name. He was not surprised to see them. Buchanan had phoned him the night before he left Boston. "Abe Harmon is down here threatening to kill you," Buchanan had said, "and I suspect you know the reason."

"Well, my dear," Pemberton said to his bride. "Our welcoming party includes some of the natives. This will make for a colorful arrival."

Pemberton took Serena's hand for a moment, felt the calluses on her upper palm, the simple gold wedding band Serena wore in lieu of a diamond. Then he stood and retrieved two grips from the overhead compartment. He handed them to the porter, who stepped back and followed as Pemberton led his bride down the aisle and the steel steps to the platform. There was a gap of two feet between the metal and wood. Serena did not reach for his hand as she stepped onto the planks. Buchanan gave a stiff formal bow. Peabody nodded and tipped his fedora.

Pemberton knew aspects of her appearance surprised his partners, not just the lack of a cloche hat and dress but her hair, blond and thick, cut short in a bob—distinctly feminine yet also austere.

Serena went to the older man and held out her hand. Pemberton noted that at five-seven his wife stood tall as Peabody.

"Peabody, I assume."

"Yes, yes, I am," he stammered.

"Serena Pemberton," she said, her hand extended so that he had no choice but to take it. She turned to the younger man.

"And Buchanan. Correct?"

"Yes," Buchanan said. He took her proffered hand and cupped it awkwardly in his.

Serena smiled slightly.

"Don't you know how to properly shake hands, Mr. Buchanan?"

Pemberton watched as Buchanan blushed and corrected his grip, withdrawing his hand quickly as he could. In the two years Boston Timber Company had been here, Buchanan's wife had come only once, arriving in a taffeta gown that was soiled before she made it to her husband's house on the other side of the street. She spent one night and left on the morning train. Now Buchanan and his wife met once a month for a weekend in Richmond, as far south as Mrs. Buchanan would travel. Peabody's wife had never left Boston.

His partners appeared incapable of speech. Their eyes shifted to peruse the leather chaps Serena wore, the oxford shirt and black jodhpurs. Her British inflection and erect carriage confirmed that, as had their wives, she'd attended private boarding school in the Northeast. But Serena had been born in Colorado, the child of a timberman who taught her to shake hands and look men in the eye as well as to ride and hunt. The porter laid the grips on the platform and went back for the two trunks stored in the back train car.

"Any sighting of my mountain lion?" Pemberton asked.

"No," Buchanan said. "A worker found tracks on Laurel Creek he thought belonged to one, but they were a bobcat's."

Peabody turned to Serena.

"Your husband hopes to kill the last panther in these mountains, but if there is one left, it's not being very cooperative."

"We will find it, won't we, Pemberton?" Serena said.

Pemberton concurred, encircling his bride with an arm.

Serena looked over at the father and daughter, who now sat on the bench together, watchful and silent as actors awaiting their cues.

"I don't know you," she said.

The daughter continued to stare at Serena sullenly. It was the father who spoke.

"My business ain't with you. It's with him standing there beside you."

"His business is mine," Serena said, "just as mine is his."

"Not this business. It was did before you got here."

Harmon nodded at his daughter's belly, then looked back at Serena.

Buchanan and Peabody stared at Pemberton, waiting for him

to intervene. The porter set the trunks on the platform. Pemberton gave the man a quarter and dismissed him.

"You're implying she's carrying my husband's child," Serena said.

"I ain't *implying* nothing," Harmon replied.

"Then you're a lucky man," Serena said. "You'll find no better sire to breed her with." Serena turned her gaze and words to the daughter on the bench. "But that's the only one. From now on, what children Pemberton has will be with me."

Harmon pushed himself fully upright and Pemberton glimpsed the ivory handle of a bowie knife before the coat resettled over it. He wondered how a man like Harmon could possess such a fine weapon. Perhaps it was booty won in a poker game or an heirloom passed down from a more prosperous ancestor. Pemberton leaned and unclasped his calfskin grip, grabbled among its contents for the wedding present Serena had given him. He turned slightly and slipped the elk-bone hunting knife from its sheath. Harmon's large freckled hand grasped the bench edge. He leaned forward but did not rise.

Several mountaineers watched expressionlessly from the courthouse steps. The only one Pemberton recognized was a crew foreman named Chaney, an older employee who'd spent five years in prison for killing two men in a card game dispute. Chaney shared his stringhouse with his blind mother, a woman given great deference in the camp as an oracle. Pemberton was glad to have him as a witness. The workers already understood Pemberton was as strong as any of them, had learned that last September when he stripped to his waist and helped unload the sawmill's heaviest machinery. Now he'd give them something besides his strength to respect.

"Let's go home, Daddy," the daughter said, and laid her hand on her father's wrist. Harmon flicked it away as if a bothersome fly and stood up.

"God damn the both of you," he said.

Harmon opened the frock coat and freed the bowie knife from its leather sheath. The blade caught the late-afternoon sun, and for a moment it appeared the mountaineer held a glistening flame in his hand.

"Go get Sheriff McDowell," Buchanan yelled toward the courthouse steps, but none of the men moved.

Pemberton unsheathed his knife as well. He felt the elk-bone handle against his palm, its roughness all the better for clasping. For a few moments he relished the knife's balance and solidity, its blade, hilt, and handle precisely calibrated as the épées he'd fenced with at Princeton.

Buchanan made a move to step between the two men, but Pemberton waved him away with his free hand.

"This is best done now," Pemberton said to Buchanan. He glanced at Serena. "Better to settle it now, right?"

"Yes," Serena said. "Settle it now."

Pemberton took a calculated step toward Harmon. The old man kept the knife head high and pointed toward the sky, and Pemberton knew he had done little fighting with a blade. Pemberton took a step closer and Harmon slashed the air between them. The man's tobacco-yellowed teeth were clenched, the veins in his neck taut as guy wires. Pemberton kept his knife low and close to his side. He took another step forward and raised his left arm. The bowie knife swept forward but its arc stopped when Harmon's forearm hit Pemberton's. Harmon jerked down and the blade sliced Pemberton's forearm. Pemberton took one final step, the blade flat as he slipped it inside Harmon's coat and plunged half the blade's length into the soft flesh above Harmon's right hip bone. He grabbed Harmon's shoulder with his free hand for leverage and quickly opened a thin smile across the mountaineer's stomach. For a second there was no blood.

Harmon's knife fell clattering onto the platform. The man placed both hands on his stomach and stepped back to the bench, slowly sat down. After a few moments he lifted his hands to see the damage, and his intestines spilled in gray ropes onto his lap. Harmon stared at them, studied the inner workings of his body as if for some further verification of his fate. He raised his head a last time, leaned it back against the depot's graying boards. Pemberton watched the man's eyes. The way they clouded over was no different than any other animal he'd watched die.

Serena stood beside him now.

"Your arm," she said.

Pemberton saw that his poplin shirt was slashed below the elbow, the light blue cloth darkened by blood. Serena unclasped a silver cuff link and rolled up the shirtsleeve, examined the cut across his forearm.

"It won't need any stitches," Serena said. "Just a dressing and some iodine."

Serena picked up the bowie knife and carried it over to Harmon's daughter, who grasped her father by the shoulders as if the dead man might yet be revived. Tears flowed down the young woman's face but she made no sound.

"Here," Serena said, holding the knife by the blade. "By all rights it belongs to my husband. It's a fine knife, and you can get a good price for it if you demand one. And I would," she added. "Sell it, I mean, because that money will help when the child is born. It's all you'll ever get from my husband or me."

Harmon's daughter looked at her now, but she did not raise a hand to take the knife. Serena set it on the bench beside the younger woman and walked across the platform to stand beside her husband.

"Is my car here?" Pemberton asked Buchanan.

"Yes, but you and Mrs. Pemberton can take the train if you want to get there faster. Chaney can drive your car back."

"No," Pemberton said. "We'll take the car."

Pemberton turned to the baggage boy, who was staring at the blood pooling copiously around Harmon's feet.

"Take that trunk and put them in my car. We'll get the grips."

"Don't you think you'd better wait for Sheriff McDowell?" Buchanan asked.

"Why?" Pemberton said. "It was self-defense, a half dozen men will verify that."

The boy followed Pemberton and his bride to the Packard, where they loaded the trunk and grips in the backseat.

Pemberton was turning the key when he saw McDowell coming up the sidewalk. The sheriff wore his Sunday finery, no badge or gun visible. Pemberton pressed the starter button on the floor, then released the hand brake and drove the Packard north into the higher mountains.

WHEN THEY GOT to the camp, a youth named Parker waited on the front steps. Beside him was a cardboard box, in it a bottle of wine, meat and bread and cheese for sandwiches. Parker retrieved the grips from the car and followed Pemberton and his bride onto the porch. Pemberton unlocked the door and nodded for the young man to enter first.

"I'd carry you over the threshold," Pemberton said, "but for the arm."

Serena smiled.

"Don't worry, Pemberton. I can cross it myself."

Serena stepped inside and Pemberton followed. She examined the light switch a moment as if doubtful electricity existed in such a place. Then she turned it on.

In the front room were two captain's chairs set in front of the fireplace, off to the left a small kitchen with a stove and icebox. A table with four cane-bottom chairs stood in the corner by the front room's one window. Serena nodded and walked down the hall, glanced at the bathroom before entering the back room. She turned on the bedside lamp and sat down on the wrought iron bed, tested the mattress's firmness and seemed satisfied. Parker appeared at the doorway, a trunk that had formerly belonged to Pemberton's father in his grasp.

"That one in the hall closet," Pemberton said. "Put the other at the foot of the bed."

The youth did as he was told and soon brought the second trunk, then the food and wine.

"Mr. Buchanan thought you might be needing something to eat," Parker said.

"Put it in the icebox," Pemberton said. "Then go get iodine and gauze from the caboose."

The youth paused, his eyes on Pemberton's blood-soaked sleeve.

"You wanting me to get Dr. Carlyle?"

"No," Serena said. "I'll dress it."

WHEN THE BOY had delivered the iodine and the gauze, Serena sat on the bed and unbuttoned Pemberton's shirt. She removed the knife and sheath wedged behind his belt buckle, took the knife from the sheath with her left hand, and examined the dried blood before placing it on the bed.

She opened the bottle of iodine.

"What was it like, killing someone with a knife?" she said.

"Like fencing, but more intimate."

"You've never killed a man like that before?"

Serena gripped his arm harder, poured the auburn-colored liquid into the wound.

"No," Pemberton said. "The other time was with fists and a beer stein. But they both had certain satisfactions."

Once Serena finished wrapping the gauze around Pemberton's wound, she picked up the knife and took it into the kitchen, wiped it clean in the basin with water, soap, and a washcloth. She dried the knife with a hand towel and returned to the back room. She set the knife and sheath on the bedside table.

"I'll take a whetstone and sharpen the blade tomorrow," Serena said. "Will you store it with your hunting equipment?"

"No," Pemberton said. "I'll keep it in the office, close at hand."

Serena sat down in a ladder-back chair opposite the bed and pulled off her jodhpurs. She undressed, not looking at what she unfastened and let fall to the floor but directly at Pemberton. She took off her underclothing and stood before him. Her eyes had not left his the whole time. The women he'd known before Serena had been shy with their bodies, waiting for a room to darken or sheets to be pulled up, but that wasn't Serena's way.

She did not come to him immediately, and a sensual languor settled over Pemberton. He gazed at her body, into the eyes that had entranced him the first time he'd met her, gray irises the color of burnished pewter. Hard and dense like pewter too, the gold flecks not so much within the gray as floating motelike on the surface. Eyes that did not close when their bodies came together.

Serena opened the curtains so moonlight could fall across the bed. She turned from the window and looked around the room, as if for a moment she'd forgotten where she was.

"This will do fine for us," she said, returning her gaze to Pemberton as she stepped toward the bed.

THE FOLLOWING MORNING Pemberton introduced his bride to the camp's workers. Serena stood beside her husband as he spoke, wearing riding breeches and a flannel shirt. Her boots were different from the ones the day before, the leather on these scuffed and worn, the toes rimmed with tarnished silver. Serena held the reins of the Morgan she'd had freighted down from Massachusetts, the horse's white coloration so intense as to appear nearly translucent in the day's first light.

"Mrs. Pemberton's father owned the Vulcan Lumber Company in Colorado," Pemberton said. "He taught her well. She's the equal of any man here, and you'll soon find the truth of it. Her orders are to be followed the same way you'd follow mine."

Among the gathered workers was a thick-bearded cutting crew foreman named Hartley. He hocked audibly and spit a gob of phlegm on the ground. At six-two and well over two hundred pounds, Hartley was one of the few men big as Pemberton in camp. Serena opened the saddlebag and removed a Waterman pen and a small spiral pad. She spoke to the horse quietly, then dropped the reins and walked over to Hartley, stood exactly where he had spit. She pointed toward the office, where a cane ash tree had been left standing for its shade.

"I will make a wager with you," Serena said to Hartley. "We'll estimate total board feet of that cane ash. Then we'll write our estimates on a piece of paper and see who's closest."

Hartley stared at Serena a few moments, then at the tree, as if already measuring its height and width. He was not looking at her when he spoke.

"How we going to know who's closest?"

"I'll have it cut down and taken to the sawmill in Waynesville. Soon as we've made our estimates."

By this time Buchanan and Dr. Carlyle had come out of the office and watched as well.

"How much we wagering?" Hartley asked.

"Two weeks' pay."

The amount gave Hartley pause.

"There ain't no trick to it? I win I get two weeks' extra pay."

"Correct," Serena said. "And if you lose you work two weeks for free."

She offered the pad and pen to Hartley, but he did not raise a hand to take it.

A lumberman behind him snickered.

"Perhaps you want me to go first then?"

"Yeah," Hartley said after a few moments.

Serena turned toward the tree and studied it almost a minute before lifting the pen with her left hand, writing down her number. She tore the page out of the pad and folded it.

"Your turn," she said and handed pad and pen to Hartley. He walked up to the cane ash to better judge its girth, then came back and looked at the tree awhile longer before writing down his own number.

AT DINNERTIME, EVERY worker in camp gathered in front of the office. The Pembertons and their partners were there as well, watching from the porch as a sawmill boss named Campbell mounted the ash tree's stump and took a pad from his coat pocket, announced the estimates and then the total board feet.

"Mrs. Pemberton the winner by thirty board feet," Campbell said, and he stepped down without further comment.

The workers began to disperse up the ridge to their string-houses, those who had bet and won stepping more lightly than the losers. As Pemberton followed their progress, he saw Mrs. Chaney on her porch. Her white hair was knotted in a tight bun and she wore a black front-buttoned dress Pemberton suspected was sewn in the previous century. She raised her milky eyes and though he knew the old woman was blind, Pemberton could not shake the sense that she was staring directly at him. *She can see things other folks can't,* Pemberton had heard one worker tell another, *and she don't need eyes to do it.*

"Time for dinner," Buchanan announced, "and a celebratory drink of our best scotch."

He and Peabody followed Carlyle and the Pembertons through the office and into the small back room whose sole furnishings were a bar on one wall and a fourteen-foot dining table, a dozen well-padded captain's chairs surrounding it. They had barely sat down when Campbell, who'd been bent over the adding machine in the office, appeared at the door. He did not speak until Pemberton asked if there was a problem.

"I just need to know if you and Mrs. Pemberton are going to hold Hartley to the bet." He gestured behind him. "For the payroll."

"Is there a reason we shouldn't?"

"He has a wife and three children."

The words were delivered with no inflection and Campbell's face was an absolute blank. Pemberton wondered, not for the first time, what it would be like to play poker with this man.

"His having a family is all for the better," Pemberton said. "It will make a more effective lesson for the other workers."

"Will he still be a foreman?" Campbell asked.

"What do you think?" Pemberton asked his bride.

"Yes," Serena replied. "For the next two weeks. Then he'll be fired. Another lesson for the men."

Campbell nodded and stepped back into the office, closing the door behind him. A few moments later the clacking, ratchet, and pause of the adding machine resumed.

Pemberton turned to Carlyle.

"I understand we had another rattlesnake bite today."

"Yes," the doctor replied. "He'll live but lose his leg."

"How many men have been bitten since the camp opened?" Serena asked.

"Five before today," Buchanan said. "Only one has died, but every man who's been bitten save one had to be let go."

The doctor turned to Serena.

"A timber rattlesnake's venom destroys blood vessels and tissue. Even if the victim is fortunate enough to survive the initial bite, lasting damage is often incurred."

"I am aware of what happens when someone is bitten by a rattlesnake, Doctor," Serena said. "Out west we have diamondbacks, which are even deadlier."

Carlyle gave a brief half bow in Serena's direction.

"I yield to the lady's superior knowledge."

Peabody, who'd seemed lost in some internal reverie, spoke.

"The rattlesnakes cost us money, and not just when a crew is halted by a bite. Men get overcautious, and progress is slowed."

"The snakes are a problem," Serena said, "and so they must be killed off, especially in the slash."

Peabody frowned.

"Yet that is the hardest place to see them, Mrs. Pemberton. They blend so well with brush and limbs as to be invisible."

"Better eyes are needed then," Serena said.

"Cold weather will be here soon and will send them up into the rock cliffs," Buchanan said.

"Until spring," Peabody said. "Then they'll be back, every bit as bad as before."

"Perhaps not," Serena said.

II

It was in early spring that Harmon's daughter returned to camp. By then Boston Lumber Company had become Pemberton Lumber Company. Peabody had suffered a stroke during a Christmas visit to New England, allowing the Pembertons to buy his share. In February, Pemberton and Buchanan went bear hunting alone near the headwaters of Hazel Creek. Buchanan had been shot. An *accident,* Pemberton had claimed, but Sheriff McDowell had been openly skeptical.

It was Campbell who told Pemberton about Harmon's daughter.

"She's sitting there in the dining hall," Campbell said. "She wants her old job in the kitchen back."

"Where has she been all this time?" Pemberton asked.

"Living with her sister over in Cullowhee the last eight months. But now she's moved back into her daddy's place on Colt Ridge."

"I don't know where that is," Pemberton said.

"No more than a mile west of here," Campbell said.

Pemberton raised himself from his office chair, looked out the window toward the dining hall.

"Does she have a child with her?"

"No," Campbell said.

"She say anything about having a child?"

"No, but I seen her in town last week and she had one with her."

"Boy or girl?"

"Looked to be a boy."

"Who's going to look after that baby if she's working?" Pemberton asked.

"Her aunt lives up there on Colt Ridge. She may be of a mind to have her look after it."

Pemberton turned from the window, sat back down.

"She was a good worker before she left last summer," Campbell added.

Pemberton looked at the man. Like so many of the highlanders, Campbell tended to never quite come out and say what he meant, or wanted. But Campbell was an intelligent man, brilliant in his way. He could fix any piece of equipment in the camp or at the sawmill, and his suggestions on new hires were invaluable.

"You know she claims that child is mine," Pemberton said.

Campbell nodded.

"You think I owe her a job because of that, or because I killed her father?"

"That ain't for me to think," Campbell said. "All I'm saying is she's a good worker."

Pemberton pushed some papers farther toward the center of his desk. "I'll have to talk with Mrs. Pemberton first."

"You want me to tell her to stay?" Campbell asked.

"Yes, I'll be back in an hour."

Pemberton got his horse and rode up the skid trail that crossed Davidson Branch and on through the stumps and slash to the wood's edge, where Serena sat on her horse, giving instructions to a cutting crew. The men slumped in various attitudes of repose, but they were attentive. When she'd finished Pemberton rode over to her.

Serena nodded at the crew as they prepared to cut a looming tulip poplar.

"The men say winter's almost over now."

"I suspect it is."

"We've done well then. Twenty men lost out of a hundred and ten. I'll take that any winter."

"Especially this one. Campbell claims he's never seen a worse one."

Serena's horse stamped impatiently.

"What brings you out this morning, Pemberton?"

"Harmon's daughter is in the dining hall. She wants her old job back."

Serena leaned slightly forward, her left hand stroking the Morgan's neck. The horse calmed.

"What kind of worker was she in the past?"

"Good."

"And given no favors because you bedded her?"

"Not then nor will she now."

"What of her child? I assume that it's alive."

"Campbell saw her with a child in town."

"What I said to her at the depot, about her getting nothing else from us."

"Yes, same wages as before."

Serena's eyes were full upon him now.

"The child. It won't be living in camp. Correct?"

"She'll live in her father's house, not one of ours."

"And when she works, who will keep the child?"

"Campbell said an aunt will take him in."

"Him. A male then."

"Campbell said so."

The sawing paused for a few moments as the lead chopper

placed another wedge behind the blade. The Morgan stamped the ground again and Serena tightened her fist around the reins.

"You be the one to tell her that she's hired," Serena said. "Just make it clear she has no claim on us. Her son either. Nothing ours is his. We will have our own child soon enough."

Pemberton nodded and shifted his weight in the saddle. The crosscut saw resumed, the blade's rapid back-and-forth like inhalations and exhalations, a sound as if the tree itself were panting.

"One other thing," Serena said. "Make sure she's not allowed around our food. She might attempt to poison you. Or me."

Serena turned the horse and made her way through drifts of fallen wood toward the crew.

When Pemberton got back to the camp he went into the dining hall, where Harmon's daughter waited. She wore a pair of polished but well-worn black oxford shoes and a blue and white calico dress Pemberton suspected was the nicest piece of clothing she owned. When he'd had his say Pemberton asked if she understood.

"Yes sir," she said.

"And what happened with your father. You saw it yourself, so you know I was defending myself."

A few moments of silence passed between them. She finally nodded, not meeting his eyes. Pemberton tried to remember what had attracted him to her in the first place. Perhaps her blue eyes and blond hair. Perhaps that she'd been the only woman at the camp who wasn't already haggard. Aging in these mountains, especially among the women, happened early. Pemberton had seen women twenty-five here who would pass for fifty in Boston.

She kept her head slightly bowed as he studied her mouth and chin, her waist and the white length of ankle showing below her threadbare dress. Whatever had attracted him to her was now gone. Attraction to every other woman besides Serena as well, he suddenly realized. He could not remember the last time he'd thought of a past consort, or watched a young beauty in Boston or Waynesville and imagined what her body would be like joined to his. He knew such constancy was rare, and before meeting Serena would have believed it impossible. Now it seemed inevitable, wondrous but also disconcerting in its finality.

"You can start tomorrow," Pemberton said.

She got up to leave and was almost to the door when he stopped her.

"The child, what's his name?"

"Esau," she said. "It comes from the Bible."

Pemberton nodded, and Harmon's daughter took this as a sign she was excused. The name was typical of the mountain people, particularly in its Old Testament derivation. Campbell's first name was Ezekiel and there was an Absalom and a Solomon in the camp. But no Lukes or Matthews, which Buchanan had once noted to Dr. Carlyle. Carlyle's response had been that the highlanders tended to live more by the Old Testament than the New.

THE EAGLE ARRIVED the following week. Serena had notified the depot master it would be coming and must be brought immediately to camp, and so it was, the six-foot-by-six-foot wooden crate and its inhabitant placed on a flatcar with two youths in attendance, the train making a slow trek up from Waynesville as if delivering a visiting dignitary.

The bird's arrival was an immediate source of rumor and speculation, especially among the crews. The men had come out of the dining hall to watch the two boys lift their charge off the flatcar, the youths solemn and ceremonious as they carried the crate into the stable.

Serena had them place the eagle in the back stall, where Campbell had built a block perch out of wood and steel and sisal rope. Serena then dismissed the two boys and they walked out of the stable side by side, each matching his stride to his fellow's. They marched back to the waiting train, eyes straight ahead and impervious to the men who implored them to tell what they knew of the eagle's sudden appearance. The boys climbed onto the flatcar and sat with legs crossed and faces shorn of expression, much in the manner of the Buddha. Several workers had followed them, but the youths ignored all imprecations. Only when the train wheels began rolling did the two boys allow themselves tight-lipped condescending smiles aimed at the lesser mortals still clamoring and running after them—the preterite who could never be entrusted as the guardians of things original and rare.

Serena and Pemberton remained in the stable, standing outside the stall door.

"You starve the bird, then what?" Pemberton said.

"She takes food from my glove," Serena replied. "But only when she's bowed and bared her neck is she truly mine. That's when I'll know she trusts me with her life."

For the next three days Serena spent all day and much of the night inside the stall with the bird. On the third afternoon Serena came to the office.

"Come and see," she told Pemberton, and they walked out to

the stable. The eagle stood on its perch, hooded and still until it heard Serena's voice. Then the bird's head swiveled in her direction. Serena stepped inside the stall and removed the hood, then placed a piece of red meat on her gauntlet and held out her arm. The eagle stepped onto Serena's forearm, gripping the goatskin as the head bowed to tear and swallow the meat between its talons.

Each morning in the following two weeks, Serena walked into the stable's back stall and freed the eagle from the block perch. She and the bird spent their mornings alone below Half Acre Ridge, where Boston Lumber had done its first cutting. For the first four days she would ride out at dawn with the eagle traveling behind her in an old applecart, a blanket draped over the cage. By the fifth day the bird perched on Serena's right forearm, its head black-hooded like an executioner, the five-foot leash tied to Serena's upper right elbow and the leather bracelets around the raptor's feet. Campbell constructed an armrest out of a Y-shaped white oak branch and affixed it to the saddle pommel. From a certain angle, the eagle itself appeared mounted on the saddle, from a distance as if horse, eagle, and human had transmogrified into some winged six-legged creature from the old primal myths.

In mid-April Campbell killed a timber rattlesnake while surveying on Shanty Mountain. The next afternoon Serena freed the eagle from the block perch and rode west to Fork Ridge, where Chaney and his crew ascended the near slope. The day was warm and many of the men worked shirtless. They did not cover themselves when Serena appeared, for they had learned she didn't care.

Serena loosed the leather laces and removed the eagle's hood, then freed the leash from the bracelets. She raised her right arm slightly. As if performing some violent salute, Serena thrust her forearm and the eagle upward. The bird ascended and began a di-hedral circle over the twenty acres of stumps behind Chaney's crew. On the third circle the eagle stopped. For a moment the bird hung poised in the sky, seemingly outside the world's slow turn-ing. Then it appeared not so much to fall but to slice open the air as if bound to some greater thing that propelled it downward. Once on the ground among the stumps and slash, the eagle opened its wings like a flourished cape. The bird wobbled forward, paused, and moved forward again, the yellow talons sparring with some creature hidden in the detritus. In another minute the eagle's head dipped, then rose with a piece of stringy pink flesh in its beak.

Serena opened her saddlebag and removed a metal whistle and a lariat. Fastened to one end of the hemp was a piece of bloody beef. She blew the whistle and the bird's neck whirled in her direc-tion as Serena swung the lure overhead.

"They Lord God," a worker said as the eagle rose, for in its talons was a three-foot-long rattlesnake. The bird flew toward the ridge crest, then arced back, drifting down toward Serena and Chaney's crew. Except for Chaney, the men scattered as if dyna-mite had been lit, stumbling and tripping over stumps and slash as they fled. The eagle settled on the ground with an elegant awk-wardness, the reptile still writhing but its movements only a mem-ory of when it had been alive. Serena got off the stallion and offered the gobbet of meat. The bird released the snake and pounced on the beef. When it had finished eating, Serena placed the hood back over the eagle's head.

"Can I have the skin and rattles?" Chaney asked.

"Yes," Serena said, "but the meat belongs to the bird, so bring the guts back to camp."

Chaney set his boot heel on the serpent's head and detached the body with a quick sweep of his barlow knife. By the time the other men returned, Chaney had finished the snake's skin folded and tucked inside his lunch box, the rattles as well.

By the following Friday the bird had killed seven rattlesnakes, including a huge satinback that panicked a crew when it slipped from the eagle's grasp midflight and fell earthward. The men had not seen the eagle overhead, and the snake fell among them like some last remnant of Satan's rebellion cast from heaven.

III

June came and Serena was now in her fifth month of pregnancy, though no one in camp other than Pemberton knew. Pemberton suspected the workers thought of Serena as beyond gender, the same as they might some natural phenomenon. Carlyle was as oblivious as the rest of the camp, reaffirming Pemberton's belief that the doctor's medical knowledge was mediocre at best.

It was dusk when Pemberton returned from looking at a twenty-thousand-acre tract in Jackson County. Light filtered through the office's one window, and Pemberton found Campbell inside working on payroll. The light in the back room was off.

"Where's Mrs. Pemberton?"

Campbell finished ratcheting a number and looked up.

"She went on up to the house."

"Has she eaten?"

Campbell nodded.

"You want me to have somebody bring you a supper up to the house?"

"No," Pemberton said. "I'll tell them."

Though it was after seven, the lights remained on in the dining room. From inside the building's oak walls came a ragged choir of voices singing a hymn. Pemberton stepped onto the porch and opened the door that led to the kitchen. The kitchen itself was deserted, despite pots left on the Burton grange stove, soiled dishes piled beside sixty-gallon hoop barrels filled with gray water.

Pemberton stepped into the dining room, where Reverend Bolick's sonorous voice had replaced the singing. Workers filled the benches set before the long wooden tables, women and children in front, men in the rear closest to where Pemberton stood. A number of workers glanced back but quickly returned their gazes to where Reverend Bolick stood behind two narrow, nailed-together vegetable crates, which resembled not so much a podium as an altar. Upon it lay a huge leather-bound Bible whose wide pages sprawled off both sides of the wood.

Pemberton scanned the benches looking for his cook. Most of the workers had their backs to him, so he moved to the side and found the man, motioned for him to go to the kitchen. Then he looked for a server and found one, but the woman was so rapt that Pemberton was almost beside Bolick before he got her attention. The woman left her seat, made her way slowly through a bumpy aisle of knees and rumps. But Pemberton was no longer looking at her.

The child lay in his mother's lap, clothed in a gray sexless bundling. He held a hand-hewn toy train car in one hand, rolling the wooden wheels up and down his leg with a solemn deliberateness. Pemberton studied the child's features intently. Reverend

Bolick stopped speaking and the dining hall was suddenly silent. The child quit rolling the train and looked up at the preacher, then at the larger man who stood close by. For a few moments the child's dark brown eyes gazed directly at Pemberton.

The congregation shifted uneasily on the benches, many of their eyes on Pemberton as Bolick turned the Bible's pages in search of a passage. When Pemberton realized he was being watched, he made his way to the back of the hall, where the kitchen workers waited.

The cook and server went on to the kitchen, but Pemberton lingered a few more moments. Bolick found the passage he'd been searching for and looked out at his audience, settling his eyes on Pemberton. For a few seconds the only sound was a spring-back knife's soft click as a worker prepared to pare his nails while listening.

"From the book of Obadiah," Bolick said, and began reading. "The pride of thine heart hath deceived thee, thou that dwellest in the cleft of the rock, whose habitation is high, that saith in his heart, who shall bring me down."

Bolick closed the Bible with a slow and profound delicacy, as if the ink were fresh-pressed on the onionskin and susceptible to smearing.

"The word of the Lord," Bolick said.

Pemberton went to the house with his dinner. He set the dishes on the table and stepped into the bedroom. Serena was asleep and Pemberton did not wake her. Instead, he softly closed the bedroom door. He did not go to the kitchen and eat, instead went to the hall closet and opened his father's trunk, rummaged through the stocks and bonds and various other legal documents until he found the cowhide-covered photograph album his aunt had insisted he pack as well. He shut the trunk softly and walked down to the office.

Campbell still worked on the payroll but left without a word when Pemberton said he wished to be alone. Embers glowed in the hearth and Pemberton set kindling and a log on the andirons and felt the heat strengthen against his back. He opened the album, the desiccated binding creaking with each turned cardboard page. When he found a photograph of himself at ten months, he stopped turning.

WITH THE PURCHASE of the second skidder, the men now worked westward on two fronts. By June the northern crews had crossed Davidson Branch and made their way to Shanty Mountain while the crews to the south followed Straight Creek west. Recent rains had slowed the progress, not just forcing the men to slog through mud but causing more accidents as well.

On Monday morning Serena mounted the Morgan and rode out to check the work on the northern front. Chaney's crew was cutting timber on the slope after a night of heavy rain. The slanting ground made footing tenuous. To make matters more difficult, Chaney's crew had a new lead chopper, a boy of seventeen stout enough but inexperienced. Chaney was showing where to make the undercut when the boy slipped as the ax swung forward.

The blade's entry made a soft, fleshy sound as Chaney and his left hand parted. The hand fell first, hitting the ground palm down, fingers curling inward like the legs of a dying spider. Chaney backed up and leaned against the white oak, blood leaping from the upraised wrist onto his shirt and denim breeches. The other sawyer stared at Chaney's wrist, then at the severed hand as if unable to reconcile the two. The boy let the ax handle slip from his hands. The two men appeared incapable of movement, even when Chaney's legs gave way and he fell sideways into the mud.

Serena dismounted and took off her coat, revealing the condition it had concealed for over a month. She kneeled beside Chaney, quickly stripped the leather string from a boot, and tied it around the man's wrist. The blood spout became a trickle.

"Get him on the horse," Serena said.

Two men lifted their wounded foreman and held him upright on the stallion until Serena mounted behind him. She rode back to camp, one arm around Chaney's waist, pressing the man against her swollen belly.

At camp Campbell and another man lifted Chaney off the horse and carried him into Dr. Carlyle's caboose. Pemberton came in a few moments later and believed he looked at a dead man. The face was pale as chalk, and Chaney's eyes rolled as if unmoored, his breathing sharp quick pants. Carlyle emptied a bottle of iodine on the wound. He finished and checked the tourniquet.

"Damn good job whoever tied this," Carlyle said. He turned to Pemberton. "You'll have to get him to the hospital quick if you want him to have a chance." The doctor paused and looked up at Pemberton. "Do you want the bother of that or not?"

"I'll take him in my car," Campbell said before Pemberton could reply. Campbell motioned to the worker who'd helped bring Chaney in and they lifted the injured man off the table, set his arms around their shoulders, and began dragging him to the car. Only then did Chaney speak.

"I'll live," he gasped. "It's done been prophesied."

Pemberton followed the men outside. He looked for Serena and saw her riding back up the ridge where Chaney's crew waited leaderless. As Pemberton went to get his own horse, he glanced toward the stringhouses and saw Mrs. Chaney on the porch, her clouded eyes turned in the direction of all that had just transpired.

A WEEK LATER Chaney walked back into camp. He had witnessed enough men hurt to know Pemberton Lumber Company took no charity cases, especially when every day men arrived begging for work. Pemberton assumed Chaney had come to get his mother, take her back to their old home on Cove Creek. But when Chaney came to his stringhouse, he did not pause but kept walking out of the camp and across the ridge to where the timber crews worked. For a few moments Pemberton contemplated the possibility that Chaney planned to avenge the loss of his left hand. That would not be a bad thing since it might make other workers more careful in the future.

Pemberton was in the back room with Dr. Carlyle when Chaney returned, walking beside Serena and the stallion. It was almost full dark and Pemberton had been watching out the window for her. She was later than usual. The food had been brought, and Carlyle had already eaten. Serena and Chaney walked toward the stable, Chaney adjusting his gait so he stayed between the saddle and the horse's rump.

They came out a few minutes later, Chaney still lagging behind Serena in the manner of a dog taught to heel. She spoke briefly to the man, who then walked toward the stringhouse where his mother was.

"We need to keep Chaney on the payroll," Serena said as she sat down at the dinner table.

"What good will he do for us with just one hand?" Pemberton asked.

"Anything I bid him do."

Dr. Carlyle looked up from his supper.

"Because you saved his life?" he asked. "As one who has saved numerous lives, dear lady, I can assure you such gratitude is fleeting."

"Not in this instance," Serena said. "His mother prophesied a time when he would lose much but be saved."

Carlyle smiled.

"No doubt a reference to some brush arbor meeting where his soul would be saved for the contents of his billfold."

"Saved by a woman," Serena added, "and thus honor bound to protect that woman and do her bidding the rest of his life."

"And you believe you are that woman?" Dr. Carlyle said. "I assumed you one to deny belief in augury."

"I don't believe in it," Serena said, "but Chaney does."

IV

In her eighth month Serena awoke with pain in her lower abdomen. Pemberton found Carlyle in the caboose ministering to a worker who had a three-inch splinter embedded in the sclera of his eye. The doctor used a pair of tweezers to work the splinter free, washed the wound out with disinfectant, and sent the man back to his crew.

"Probably something has not lain on her stomach well," Carlyle said as they walked to the house.

Chaney waited on the porch, Serena's horse saddled and tethered to the lower banister.

"Mrs. Pemberton will be staying in today," Pemberton said.

Chaney gazed steadily at Carlyle's black physician's bag as the two men passed and went on in the house.

Serena sat on the bed edge. Her face was pale, and her slow, shallow breaths were such as one might use while holding something incredibly fragile or incredibly dangerous. Serena's peignoir lay open, the dark-blue silk rippling back to reveal her waxing belly.

"Lie down on your back," Carlyle said, and took a stethoscope from his bag. The doctor pressed the instrument to Serena's stomach and listened a few moments.

"All is well, madam."

The doctor smiled at Serena.

"It is normal for women to be susceptible to minor, sometimes even nonexistent pains, especially when with child. What you are feeling is probably a mild gastrointestinal upset, or to put it less delicately, excessive gas."

"Mrs. Pemberton is no hypochondriac," Pemberton said as Serena slowly raised herself to a sitting position.

"I do not mean to imply such," Dr. Carlyle said. "The mind is its own place, as the poet tells us. What one feels one feels. Therein it has its own peculiar reality."

Pemberton watched Carlyle flatten his hand as if preparing to pat his patient on the shoulder, but the doctor wisely reconsidered and let the hand remain by his side.

"I can assure you that she will be better by morning," Dr. Carlyle said when they stepped back out on the porch.

"Is there anything that will help until then?" Pemberton asked. He nodded at Chaney, who still waited on the steps. "Chaney can go to the commissary, to town if necessary."

"Yes," Dr. Carlyle said, then turned to Chaney. "Go to the commissary and fetch your mistress a bag of peppermints. I find they do wonders when my stomach is sour."

THE NEXT MORNING Pemberton awoke to find his wife sitting up with the covers at her feet, Serena's open left hand pressed between her legs. When he asked what was wrong, Serena could not speak. Instead, she raised the hand as if making a vow, her fingers and palm slick with blood. He lifted Serena into his arms and carried her out the door. The train was about to make an early run to the sawmill and men had collected around the tracks. Pemberton yelled at several loitering workers to uncouple all the cars but for the coach. Mud holes pocked the ground but Pemberton stumbled right through them as men scurried to uncouple cars and the fireman frantically shoveled coal. Campbell had come from the office and helped get Serena into the coach and lay her across a seat. Pemberton told the highlander to call the hospital and have a doctor and ambulance waiting at the depot, then to drive Pemberton's Packard to the hospital. Campbell left and Pemberton and Serena were alone amidst the shouts of workers and the Shay engine's gathering racket.

Pemberton sat on the seat edge and pressed a towel against Serena's groin to try to stanch the bleeding. Serena's eyes were closed, her face fading to the pallor of marble as the engineer put the reverser into forward. The tumbler shaft turned and set the position of the steam valves. The engineer knocked off the brakes and opened up the throttle. Pemberton listened to the train make its gradations toward motion, steam entering the throttle valve into the admission pipes and into the cylinders before the push of the pistons against the rod, and the rod turning the crankshaft and then the line shaft turning through the universal joints and the pinion gears meshing with the bull gears. Only then the wheels ever so slowly coming alive.

Pemberton opened his eyes and looked out the window and it was as if the train were crossing the bottom of a deep clear lake, everything slowed by the density of water—Campbell entered the office to call the hospital, workers came out of the dining hall to watch the engine and lead car pull away. Chaney emerged from the stable, his half arm flopping uselessly as he ran after the train.

By the time the train pulled into the depot, the towel was saturated. Serena had not made a sound the whole way, and now she'd lapsed into unconsciousness. Two orderlies in white helped Serena off the train and into the waiting ambulance. Pemberton and the hospital doctor got in as well. The doctor, a man in his early eighties known for his bluntness, lifted the soggy towel and cursed.

"Why in God's name wasn't she brought sooner?" the doctor said. "She's going to need blood, a lot of it and fast. What's her blood type?"

Pemberton did not know and Serena was past telling anyone.

"Same as mine," Pemberton said.

Once in the hospital emergency room, Pemberton and Serena lay side by side on metal gurneys, thin feather pillows cushioning their heads. The doctor rolled up Pemberton's sleeve and shunted his forearm with the needle, then did the same to Serena. They were connected now by three feet of rubber hose, the olive-shaped pump blooming in the tubing's center. The doctor squeezed the pump. Satisfied, he motioned for the nurse to take it and stand in the narrow space between the gurneys.

"Every thirty seconds," the doctor told her. "Any faster and the vein can collapse."

The doctor stepped around the gurney to minister to Serena as the nurse squeezed the rubber pump, checked the wall clock until half a minute passed, and squeezed again.

Pemberton raised his shunted arm and gripped the nurse's wrist with his hand.

"I'll pump the blood," he said.

"I don't think . . ." the nurse said.

Pemberton tightened his grip, enough that the nurse gasped. She opened her hand and let him take the pump.

Pemberton watched the clock and when fifteen seconds had passed he squeezed the rubber. He did so again, listening for the hiss and suck of his blood passing through the tube. But there was no sound, just as there was no way to see his blood coursing through the dark-gray tubing. Each time he squeezed, Pemberton closed his eyes so he could imagine the blood pulsing from his arm into Serena's and from there up through the vein and into her heart, imagined the heart itself expanding as it refilled with blood.

Pemberton turned his head toward her. He listened to her soft inhalations and matched his breathing exactly to hers. He became light-headed, no longer able to focus enough to read the clock or follow the words passing between the doctor and nurses. Pemberton squeezed the pump, his hand unable to close completely around it. He listened to his and Serena's one breath, even as he felt the needle being pulled from his forearm, heard the wheels of Serena's gurney as it rolled away. He still heard their one breath, the pulsing engine of blood inside their veins.

PEMBERTON WAS STILL on the gurney when he awoke. The doctor loomed above, an orderly beside him.

"Let us help you up," the doctor said, and the two men raised Pemberton to a sitting position. He felt the room darken for a few moments, then lighten.

"Where is Serena?" he asked. The words came out halting and raspy, as if he had not spoken in months. He directed his eyes toward the clock until he was able to focus enough to read it. Had one been on the wall, he would have checked a calendar to know the day and month. He closed his eyes a few moments and raised forefinger and thumb to the bridge of his nose. He opened his eyes and things seemed clearer.

"Where is Serena?" Pemberton said again.

"In the other wing," the doctor said.

Pemberton gripped the gurney's edge, prepared to stand up, but the orderly placed a firm hand on Pemberton's knee.

"Her constitution is quite remarkable," the doctor said, "so unless something unforeseen occurs, she'll live. But the baby is dead. And your wife's uterus, it's lacerated through the cervix."

"And that means what?" Pemberton asked.

"That you and she can have no more children."

"But she will live?"

"Yes," the doctor said. "She will live."

The orderly and doctor helped Pemberton off the gurney.

"You gave a lot of blood," the doctor said. "Too much, so be careful. You could pass out."

"Which room?" Pemberton asked.

"Forty-one," the doctor said. "Crenshaw here can go with you."

"I can find it," Pemberton said and walked slowly toward the door, past the corner table where nothing now lay.

He stepped out of the emergency room and down the corridor. The hospital's two wings were connected by the main lobby, and as Pemberton passed through he saw Campbell sitting by the front doorway. The highlander rose from his chair as Pemberton approached.

"Leave the car here for me and take the train back to camp," Pemberton said. "Make sure the crews are working and then go by the sawmill, make sure there are no problems there."

Campbell took the Packard's keys from his pocket. As Pemberton turned to leave Campbell spoke.

"If there's someone asks about how Mrs. Pemberton and the young one is doing, what do you want me to say?"

"That Mrs. Pemberton is going to be fine."

Campbell nodded but did not move.

"What else?" Pemberton asked.

"Dr. Carlyle, he rode into town with me," Campbell said.

Pemberton tried to keep his voice level.

"Where is he now?"

"I don't know. He said he was going to get Mrs. Pemberton some flowers but he ain't come back."

"How long ago was that?"

"Three hours."

"I've got some business with him I'll settle later," Pemberton said.

"You ain't the only one," Campbell said as he reached to open the door.

Pemberton stopped him with a hand on his shoulder.

"Who else?"

"Chaney. He come by a hour ago asking where Dr. Carlyle was."

Pemberton took his hand off Campbell's shoulder and the worker went on out the door. Pemberton walked across the lobby and up the opposite corridor, reading the black door numbers until he reached Serena's room.

She was still unconscious when he came in, so he pulled up a chair beside her bed and waited. As late morning and afternoon passed, Pemberton listened to her breath, watched the slow return of color to her face. The drugs kept Serena in a drifting stupor, her eyes occasionally opening but unfocused. A nurse brought him lunch and then supper. Only when the last sunlight had drained from the room's one window did Serena's eyes open and find Pemberton's. She seemed fully cognizant, which surprised the nurse because the morphine drip was still in her arm. The nurse checked the drip to make sure it was operating and then left. Pemberton turned in his chair to face her. He slid his right hand under Serena's wrist, let his fingers clasp around it like a bracelet.

She turned her head to better see him, her words a whisper.

"The child is dead?"

"Yes."

Serena studied Pemberton's face a few moments.

"What else?"

"We won't be able to have another child."

She remained silent a few moments, and Pemberton wondered if the drugs were taking hold again but then Serena spoke.

"Better this way, just us. We should have known so from the very start."

Pemberton nodded and squeezed Serena's wrist, felt again the strong pulse of their blood.

V

On an evening three weeks later the sun's last light soaked into the western ridgetops. Night thickened but offered no stars, only a rising moon pale as bone. Pemberton and Serena ate alone in the office's back room. Serena had ridden out to supervise the crews for five days now. Her face was haggard evenings when she returned, but the clothes no longer hung loose. She'd taken the eagle with her that morning, which Pemberton believed the surest sign of her recovery.

When they'd finished their coffee, Pemberton pushed back his chair and stood but Serena remained seated.

"I have a bit more work to do tonight."

"I or we?"

"I," Serena said.

"And it can't wait till morning?"

"No, better to go ahead and get it done."

"You're not well yet," Pemberton said. "Not completely."

Serena rose and came around the table and stood before him. She reached her hand behind Pemberton's head, clutching his hair as she pressed his mouth to hers. She held the kiss, settled her free hand on his lower back and pressed him closer. A full minute passed before she stepped away.

"Still believe I'm not completely well, Pemberton?"

"I'm convinced," he said. "But still . . ."

"Go on to the house," Serena said. "Chaney will be around if I need help."

Serena took him by the upper arm, led him toward the office.

"Go on, Pemberton," she said softly. "I'll join you in just a little while."

Chaney waited on the porch. As soon as Pemberton went by, Chaney stepped into the office, where Serena had remained. Pemberton walked past Dr. Carlyle's house, empty since its former inhabitant was found in the Asheville train station's bathroom with a peppermint between his death-locked teeth. Pemberton mounted the steps to his house and went inside. A counteroffer for the Jackson County tract lay on the kitchen table. He sat down and began to read.

When an hour had gone by Pemberton left the kitchen and stood on the front porch. The office lights were off, dark in the barn and stable as well. He walked over to the porch edge, stared up the ridge and found Chaney's stringhouse. It was dark. Just as Pemberton was about to go back inside, the moon emerged from behind a cloud. The first full moon of October, what the mountaineers called a hunter's moon, and at the same moment a stooped figure emerged on Chaney's porch like something rising out of deep water. The old woman faced not toward the camp but westward.

Serena returned at dawn. She undressed and got in bed, pressed her body against Pemberton's. He felt the night's chill in the hand she rested on his side. Serena's lips lightly touched his, then she settled her head into the feather pillow and slept.

THE FOLLOWING AFTERNOON Sheriff McDowell knocked on the office door and waited for Pemberton to acknowledge him before entering. Pemberton motioned for the sheriff to come in. He did not offer the man a seat, nor did the sheriff ask for one.

"What brings you to the camp that a telephone call couldn't convey, Sheriff McDowell?" Pemberton said, looking over at the clock for emphasis. "I've got too much work to entertain uninvited guests."

McDowell did not speak until Pemberton's gaze again focused on him.

"Sarah Harmon and her son were found in the river this morning."

The sheriff's eyes absorbed Pemberton's surprise.

The only sound for a few moments was the Franklin clock ticking on the credenza.

"So they drowned?" Pemberton asked.

"The mother did, or so Saul Parton claims, though he's not filling out his coroner's report until someone from Raleigh has a look at her."

"And the child?"

"His throat was cut. Left to right, so whoever did it was a lefty."

Pemberton told himself not to look in the direction of the gun rack until McDowell was out of the office. What else not to do, he asked himself, but could think of nothing else. He checked the clock but the minute hand had not moved.

"How long were the bodies in the water?" Pemberton said.

"Parton believes since around midnight."

"Perhaps the river caused the cut throat," Pemberton said. "That river is rocky and fast. A body could be tumbled about, cut by a sharp rock."

The sheriff looked at the floor a few moments as if studying the grain of the wood. He slowly raised his eyes to look directly at Pemberton.

"Do you think we're utter fools down here?" McDowell said. "Or just so afraid we'll let you do anything?"

Pemberton resisted the urge to answer.

"I went over to Asheville last week," McDowell continued. "It's not my jurisdiction but I talked to the coroner about Carlyle. He said once he got Carlyle's clothes off he found five possible causes of death. Whoever killed Carlyle had it in for him. I can't do anything about Abe Harmon or Buchanan or Carlyle, but I vow I'll do something about the murder of a mother and her child."

McDowell paused, his voice softer, more reflective.

"There's something about it," he said, "seeing a child laid out in a morgue. It takes root in the mind and nothing can get it out."

McDowell splayed his fingers and ran them through his hair, revealing a few streaks of silver Pemberton had not noticed before. He had no idea how old the man was, though he would have guessed forty-five, maybe fifty.

"When was the last time you saw that child?" McDowell asked, looking at Pemberton now.

"Are you expecting me to say last night, Sheriff?"

McDowell waited.

"June. She brought him to one of Bolick's services."

"I seen him about that time as well. He'd grown a lot since then. His face had filled out more, become a lot more like yours."

McDowell paused, then stared into Pemberton's eyes as if trying to look through them deep into the brain that lay behind.

"The eye color too," he said softly, "not blue like his mama's but molasses brown, not a whit's difference between that child's eyes and the eyes I'm looking at right now."

"I've got work to do, Sheriff," Pemberton said. He peered at an invoice on the desk, raised it slightly as if to better read the numbers.

"I measured a boot print left on the sandbar," McDowell said. "A distinctive type of boot from the narrow toe, nothing you'd buy around here. From the size and shape I'm betting it's a woman's. Now all I've got to do is find my Cinderella."

Pemberton did not raise his eyes from the invoice but knew the sheriff watched for a reaction. After a few more moments McDowell turned and walked out the door. Pemberton watched from his window as the sheriff got in his car and drove back across the ridge toward Waynesville. He locked the office door and went to the gun rack, opened the drawer beneath the mounted rifles.

The hunting knife was in the same place as before, but when he pulled it from the sheath blood stained the blade. The blood was black and appeared to be clotted, but when Pemberton scratched a fleck free and rubbed it between his thumb and forefinger, he felt a residue of moisture.

The phone rang and Pemberton picked it up. Campbell was calling from the sawmill. Almost all the train cars had been loaded. Pemberton's voice seemed hardly a part of him as he told Campbell he'd be there in a few minutes.

He hung up the phone. The knife lay on the desk, and Pemberton picked it up.

He considered taking the knife to the sawmill and throwing it in the splash pond. He realized that for the first time in memory he felt vulnerable, almost afraid. For a few moments he did nothing. Then Pemberton rubbed the blade clean with a handkerchief, slid the knife in the sheath, and returned it to the gun rack's drawer.

❖

PUBLISHER'S NOTE:

The story "Speckled Trout," which won a 2005 O. Henry Award, was later altered and extended to become the 2006 novel *The World Made Straight*. What follows is the story in its original form.

Speckled Trout

Lanny came upon the marijuana plants while fishing Caney Creek. It was a Saturday, and after helping his father sucker tobacco all morning, he'd had the truck and the rest of the afternoon and evening for himself. He'd changed into his fishing clothes and driven the three miles of dirt road to the French Broad. He drove fast, the rod and reel clattering side to side in the truck bed and clouds of red dust rising in his wake. He had the windows down and if the radio worked he'd have had it blasting. The driver's license in his billfold was six months old but only in the last month had his daddy let him drive the truck by himself.

He parked by the bridge and walked upriver toward where

Caney Creek entered. Afternoon sunlight slanted over Brushy Mountain and tinged the water the deep gold of cured tobacco. A big fish leaped in the shallows, but Lanny's spinning rod was broken down and even if it hadn't been he would not have bothered to make a cast. There was nothing in the river he could sell, only stocked rainbows and browns, knottyheads, and catfish. The men who fished the river were mostly old men who stayed in one place for hours, motionless as the stumps and rocks they sat on. Lanny liked to keep moving, and he fished where even the younger fishermen wouldn't go.

In forty minutes he was half a mile up Caney Creek, the spinning rod still broken down. The gorge narrowed to a thirty-foot wall of water and rock, below it the deepest pool on the creek. This was the place where everyone else turned back. Lanny waded through waist-high water to reach the left side of the waterfall. Then he began climbing, using juts and fissures in the rock for leverage and resting places. When he got to the top he put the rod together and tied a gold Panther Martin on the line.

The only fish this far up were what fishing magazines called brook trout, though Lanny had never heard Old Man Jenkins or anyone else call them anything other than speckled trout. Jenkins swore they tasted better than any brown or rainbow and paid Lanny fifty cents apiece no matter how small they were. Old Man Jenkins ate them head and all, like sardines.

Mountain laurel slapped Lanny's face and arms, and he scraped his hands and elbows climbing straight up rocks there was no other way around. The only path was water now. He thought of his daddy back at the farmhouse and smiled to himself. The old man had told him never to fish a place like this alone, because a broken leg or a rattlesnake bite could get you stone dead before anyone found you. That was near about the only kind of talk he got anymore from the old man, Lanny thought to himself as he tested his knot, always being lectured about something—how fast he drove, who he hung out with—like he was eight years old instead of sixteen, like the old man himself hadn't raised all sorts of hell when he was young.

The only places with enough water to hold fish were the pools, some no bigger than a wash bucket. Lanny flicked the spinner into these pools and in every third or fourth one a small, orange-finned trout came flopping out onto the bank, the spinner's treble hook snagged in its mouth. Lanny would slap the speckled's head against a rock and feel the fish shudder in his hand and die. If he missed a strike, he cast again into the same pool. Unlike browns and rainbows, the speckleds would hit twice, occasionally even three times. Old Man Jenkins had told Lanny when he was a boy most every stream in the county was thick with speckleds, but they'd been too easy caught and soon enough fished out, which was why now you had to go to the back of beyond to find them.

Lanny already had eight fish in his creel when he passed the No Trespassing sign nailed in an oak tree. The sign was scabbed with rust like the ten-year-old car tag on his granddaddy's barn, and he paid no more attention to the sign than when he'd first seen it a month ago. He knew he was on Toomey land, and he knew the stories. How Linwood Toomey once used his thumb to gouge a man's eye out in a bar fight and another time opened a man's face from ear to mouth with a broken beer bottle. Stories about events Lanny's daddy had witnessed before, as his daddy put it, he'd got straight with the Lord. But Lanny had heard other things. About how Linwood Toomey and his son were too lazy and hard drinking to hold steady jobs. Too lazy and drunk to walk the quarter-mile from their farmhouse to look for trespassers, Lanny figured.

He waded on upstream, going farther than he'd ever been. He caught more speckleds, and soon ten dollars' worth bulged in his creel. Enough money for gas, maybe even a couple of bootleg beers, he told himself, and though it wasn't near the money he'd been making at the Pay-Lo bagging groceries, at least he could do this alone and not have to deal with some old bitch of a store manager with nothing better to do than watch his every move, then fire him just because he was late a few times.

He came to where the creek forked and that was where he saw a sudden high greening a few yards above him on the left. He left the water and climbed the bank to make sure it was what he thought it was. The plants were staked like tomatoes and set in rows the same way as tobacco or corn. He knew they were worth money, a lot of money, because Lanny knew how much his friend Shank paid for an ounce of pot and this wasn't just ounces but maybe pounds.

He heard something behind him and turned, ready to drop the rod and reel and make a run for it. On the other side of the creek, a gray squirrel scrambled up a blackjack oak. Lanny told himself that there was no reason to get all jumpy, that nobody would have seen him coming up the creek.

He let his eyes scan what lay beyond the plants. He didn't see anything moving, not even a cow or chicken. Nothing but some open ground and then a stand of trees. He rubbed a pot leaf between his finger and thumb, and it felt like money to him, more money than he'd make at the Pay-Lo. He looked around one more time before he took the knife from its sheath and cut down five plants. The stalks had a twiny toughness like rope.

That was the easy part. Dragging the stalks a mile down the creek was a lot harder, especially while trying to keep the leaves and buds from being stripped off. When he got to the river he hid the plants in the underbrush and walked the trail to make sure no one was fishing. Then he carried the plants to the road edge, stashed them in the ditch, and got the truck. He emptied the creel into the ditch, the trout stiff and glaze-eyed. He wouldn't be delivering Old Man Jenkins any speckleds this evening.

Lanny drove back home with the plants hidden under willow branches and potato sacks. He planned to stay only long enough to get a shower and put on some clean clothes, but as he walked through the front room his father looked up from the TV.

"We ain't ate yet."

"I'll get something in town," Lanny said.

"No, your momma's fixing supper right now, and she's set the table for three."

"I ain't got time. Shank is expecting me."

"You can make time, boy. Or I might take a notion to go somewhere in that truck myself this evening."

It was seven-thirty before Lanny drove into the Hardee's parking lot and parked beside Shank's battered Camaro. He got out of the truck and walked over to Shank's window.

"You ain't going to believe what I got in back of the truck."

Shank grinned.

"It ain't that old prune-faced bitch that fired you, is it?"

"No, this is worth something."

Shank got out of the Camaro and walked around to the truck

bed with Lanny. Lanny looked to see if anyone was watching, then lifted a sack so Shank could see one of the stalks.

"I got five of 'em."

"Shit fire, boy. Where'd that come from?"

"Found it when I was fishing."

Shank pulled the sack back farther.

"I need to start doing my fishing with you. It's clear I been going to the wrong places."

A car drove up to the drive-through and Shank pulled the sack back over the plants.

"What you planning to do with it?"

"Make some money, if I can figure out who'll buy it."

"Leonard will, I bet."

"He don't know me, though. I ain't one of his potheads."

"Well, I am," Shank said. "Let me lock my car and we'll go pay him a visit."

"How about we go over to Dink's first and get some beer."

"Leonard's got beer. His is cheaper and it ain't piss-warm like what we got at Dink's last time."

They drove out of Marshall, following 221 toward Mars Hill. The carburetor knocked and popped as the pickup struggled up Jenkins Mountain. Soon enough Lanny figured he'd have money for a kit, maybe even enough to buy a whole new carburetor.

"You in for a treat, meeting Leonard," Shank said. "They ain't another like him, leastways in this county."

"I heard tell he was a lawyer once."

"Naw, he just went to law school a few months. They kicked his ass out because he was stoned all the time."

After a mile they turned off the blacktop and onto a dirt road.

On both sides what had once been pasture was now thick with blackjack oak and briars. They passed a deserted farmhouse and turned onto another road no better than a logging trail.

The woods opened into a small meadow, at the center a battered green and white trailer, its windows painted black. On one side of the trailer a satellite dish sprouted like an enormous mushroom, on the other side a Jeep Cherokee, its back fender crumpled. Two Dobermans scrambled out from under the trailer, barking as they raced toward the truck. They leaped at Lanny's window, their claws raking the door as he quickly rolled up the window.

The trailer door opened and a man with a gray ponytail and wearing only a pair of khaki shorts stepped onto the cinder-block steps. He yelled at the dogs and when that did no good he came out to the truck and kicked at them until they slunk back from where they had emerged.

Lanny looked at a man who wasn't any taller than himself and looked to outweigh him only because of a stomach that sagged over the front of his shorts like a half-deflated balloon.

"That's Leonard?"

"Yeah. The one and only."

Leonard walked over to Shank's window.

"I got nothing but beer and a few nickel bags. Supplies are going to be low until people start to harvest."

"Well, we likely come at a good time then." Shank turned to Lanny. "Let's show Leonard what you brought him."

Lanny got out and pulled back the branches and potato sacks.

"Where'd you get that from?" Leonard asked.

"Found it," Lanny said.

"Found it, did you. And you figured finders keepers."

"Yeah," said Lanny.

Leonard let his fingers brush some of the leaves.

"Looks like you dragged it through every briar patch and laurel slick between here and the county line."

"There's plenty of buds left on it," Shank said.

"What you give me for it?" Lanny asked.

Leonard lifted each stalk, looking at it the same way Lanny had seen buyers look at tobacco.

"Fifty dollars."

"You trying to cheat me," Lanny said. "I'll find somebody else to buy it."

As soon as he spoke Lanny wished he hadn't, because he'd heard from more than one person that Leonard Hamby was a man you didn't want to get on the wrong side of. He was about to say that he reckoned fifty dollars would be fine but Leonard spoke first.

"You may have an exalted view of your entrepreneurial abilities," Leonard said.

Lanny didn't understand all the words but he understood the tone. It was smart-ass but it wasn't angry.

"I'll give you sixty dollars, and I'll double that if you bring me some that doesn't look like it's been run through a hay baler. Plus I got some cold beers inside. My treat."

"Okay," Lanny said, surprised at Leonard but more surprised at himself, how tough he'd sounded. He tried not to smile as he thought how when he got back to Marshall he'd be able to tell his friends he'd called Leonard Hamby a cheater to his face and Leonard hadn't done a damn thing about it but offer more money and free beer.

Leonard took a money clip from his front pocket and peeled off three twenties and handed them to Lanny. Leonard nodded toward the meadow's far corner.

"Put them over there next to my tomatoes. Then come inside if you got a notion to."

Lanny and Shank carried the plants through the knee-high grass and laid them next to the tomatoes. As they approached the trailer, Lanny watched where the Dobermans had vanished under it. He didn't lift his eyes until he reached the steps.

Inside, Lanny's vision took a few moments to adjust because the only light came from a TV screen. Strings of unlit Christmas lights ran across the walls and over door eaves like bad wiring. A dusty couch slouched against the back wall. In the corner Leonard sat in a fake-leather recliner patched with black electrician's tape. Except for a stereo system, the rest of the room was shelves filled with books and CDs. Music was playing, music that didn't have any guitars or words.

"Have a seat," Leonard said and nodded at the couch.

A woman stood in the foyer between the living room and kitchen. She was a tall, bony woman, and the cutoff jeans and halter top she wore had little flesh to hold them up. She'd gotten a bad sunburn and there were pink patches on her skin where she'd peeled. To Lanny she mostly looked wormy and mangy, like some stray dog around a garbage dump. Except for her eyes. They were a deep blue, like a jaybird's feathers. If you could just keep looking into her eyes, she'd be a pretty woman, Lanny told himself.

"How about getting these boys a couple of beers, Wendy," Leonard said.

"Get them your ownself," the woman said and disappeared into the back of the trailer.

Leonard shook his head but said nothing as he got up. He brought back two longneck Budweisers and a sandwich bag filled with pot and some rolling papers.

He handed the beers to Shank and Lanny and sat down. Lanny was thirsty, and he drank quickly as he watched Leonard carefully shake some pot out of the Baggie and onto the paper. Leonard licked the paper and twisted both ends, then lit it.

The orange tip brightened as Leonard drew the smoke in. He handed the joint to Shank, who drew on it as well and handed it back.

"What about your buddy?"

"He don't smoke pot. Scared his daddy would find out and beat the tar out of him."

"That ain't so," Lanny said. "I just like a beer buzz better."

Lanny lifted the bottle to his lips and drank until the bottle was empty.

"I'd like me another one."

"Quite the drinker, aren't you," Leonard said. "Just make sure you don't overdo it. I don't want you passed out and pissing on my couch."

"I ain't gonna piss on your couch."

Leonard took another drag off the joint and passed it back to Shank.

"They're in the refrigerator," Leonard said. "You can get one easy as I can."

Lanny stood up and for a moment felt off plumb, maybe because he'd drunk the beer so fast. When the world steadied he got the beer and sat back down on the couch. He looked at the TV, some kind of western but without the sound on he couldn't tell what was happening. He drank the second beer quick as the first while Shank and Leonard finished smoking the pot.

Shank had his eyes closed.

"Man, I'm feeling good," he said.

Lanny studied Leonard who sat in the recliner, trying to figure out what it was that made Leonard Hamby a man you didn't want to mess with. Leonard looked soft, Lanny thought, white and soft like bread dough. Just because a man had a couple of mean dogs didn't make him such a badass, he told himself. He thought about his own daddy and Linwood Toomey, big men you could look at and tell right away you'd not want to cross them. Lanny wondered if anyone would ever call him a badass and wished again that he didn't take after his mother, who was short and thin-boned.

"What's this shit you're listening to, Leonard?" Lanny said.

"It's called *Appalachian Spring*. It's by Copland."

"Ain't never heard of them."

Leonard looked amused.

"Are you sure? They used to be the warm-up act for Lynyrd Skynyrd."

"I don't believe that."

"No matter. Copland is an acquired taste, and I don't anticipate your listening to a classical music station any time in the future."

Lanny knew Leonard was putting him down, talking over him like he was stupid, and it made him think of his teachers at the high school, teachers who used smart-ass words against him when he gave them trouble because they were too old and scared to try anything else. He got up and made his way to the refrigerator, damned if he was going to ask permission. He got the beer out and opened the top but didn't go back to the couch. He went down the hallway to find the bathroom.

The bedroom door was open, and he could see the woman sitting on the bed reading a magazine. He pissed and then walked into the bedroom and stood next to her.

The woman laid down the magazine.

"What do you want?"

Lanny grinned.

"What you offering?"

Even buzzed up with beer, he knew it was a stupid thing to say. It seemed to him that ever since he'd got to Leonard's his mouth had been a faucet he couldn't shut off.

The woman's blue eyes stared at him like he was nothing more than a sack of shit.

"I ain't offering you anything," she said. "Even if I was, a little peckerhead like you wouldn't know what to do with it."

The woman looked toward the door.

"Leonard," she shouted.

Leonard appeared at the doorway.

"It's past time to get your Cub Scout meeting over."

Leonard nodded at Lanny.

"I believe you boys have overstayed your welcome."

"I was getting ready to leave anyhow," Lanny said. He turned toward the door and the beer slipped from his hand and spilled on the bed.

"Nothing but a little peckerhead," the woman said.

In a few moments he and Shank were outside. The evening sun glowed in the treetop like a snagged orange balloon. The first lightning bugs rode over the grass as though carried on an invisible current.

"You get more plants, come again," Leonard said and closed the trailer door.

LANNY WENT BACK the next Saturday, two burlap sacks stuffed into his belt. After he'd been fired from the Pay-Lo, he'd about given up hope on earning enough money for his own truck, but now things had changed. Now he had what was pretty damn near a money tree and all he had to do was get its leaves and buds to Leonard Hamby. He climbed up the waterfall, the trip easier without a creel and rod. Once he passed the No Trespassing sign, he moved slower, quieter. I bet Linwood Toomey didn't even plant it, Lanny told himself. I bet it was somebody who figured the Toomeys were too sorry to notice pot growing on their land.

When he came close to where the plants were, he crawled up the bank, slowly raising his head like a soldier in a trench. He scanned the tree line across the field and saw no one. He told himself even if someone hid in the trees, they could never get across the field to catch him before he was long gone down the creek.

Lanny cut the stalks just below the last leaves. Six plants filled the sacks. He thought about cutting more, taking what he had to the truck and coming back to get the rest, but he figured that was too risky. He made his way back down the creek. He didn't see anyone on the river trail, but if he had he'd have said it was poke shoots in the sacks if they'd asked.

When he drove up to the trailer, Leonard was watering the tomatoes with a hose. Leonard cut off the water and herded the Dobermans away from the truck. Lanny got out and walked around to the truck bed.

"How come you grow your own tomatoes but not your own pot?"

"Because I'm a low-risk kind of guy. Since they've started using the planes and helicopters, it's gotten too chancy unless you have a place way back in some hollow."

One of the Dobermans growled from beneath the trailer but did not show its face.

"Where's your partner?"

"I don't need no partner," Lanny said. He lifted the sacks from the truck bed and emptied them onto the ground between him and Leonard.

"That's one hundred and twenty dollars' worth," Lanny said.

Leonard stepped closer and studied the plants.

"Fair is fair," he said and pulled the money clip from his pocket. He handed Lanny five twenty-dollar bills and four fives.

Lanny crumpled the bills in his fist and stuffed them into his pocket, but he did not get back in the truck.

"What?" Leonard finally said.

"I figured you to ask me in for a beer."

"I don't think so. I don't much want to play host this afternoon."

"You don't think I'm good enough to set foot in that roachy old trailer of yours."

Leonard looked at Lanny and smiled.

"Boy, you remind me of a banty rooster, strutting around not afraid of anything, puffing your feathers out anytime anyone looks at you wrong. You think you're a genuine, hard-core badass, don't you?"

"I ain't afraid of you, if that's what you're getting at. If your own woman ain't scared of you, why should I be?"

Leonard looked at the money clip. He tilted it in his hand until the sun caught the metal and a bright flash hit Lanny in the face. Lanny jerked his head away from the glare.

Leonard laughed and put the money clip back in his pocket.

"After the world has its way with you a few years, it'll knock some of the strut out of you. If you live that long."

"I ain't wanting your advice," Lanny said. "I just want some beer."

Leonard went into the trailer and brought out a six-pack.

"Here," he said. "A farewell present. Don't bother to come around here anymore."

"What if I get you some more plants?"

"I don't think you better try to do that. Whoever's pot that is will be harvesting in the next few days. You best not be anywhere near when they're doing it either."

"What if I do get more?"

"Same price, but if you want any beer you best be willing to pay bootleg price like your buddies."

THE NEXT DAY, soon as Sunday lunch was finished, Lanny put on jeans and a T-shirt and tennis shoes and headed toward the French Broad. The day was hot and humid, and the only people on the river were a man and two boys swimming near the far bank.

By the time he reached the creek his T-shirt was soaked and sweat stung his eyes.

Upstream the trees blocked out most of the sun and the cold water he waded through cooled him. At the waterfall, an otter slid into the pool. Lanny watched its body surge through the water, straight and sleek as a torpedo, before disappearing under the far bank. He wondered how much an otter pelt was worth and figured come winter it might be worth finding out. He kneeled and cupped his hand, the pool's water so cold it hurt his teeth.

He climbed the left side of the falls, then made his way upstream until he got to the No Trespassing sign. If someone waited for him, Lanny believed that by now the person would have figured out he'd come up the creek, so he stepped up on the right bank and climbed the ridge into the woods. He followed the sound of water until he figured he'd gone far enough and came down the slope slow and quiet, stopping every few yards to listen. When he got to the creek, he looked upstream and down before crossing.

The plants were still there. He pulled the sacks from his belt and walked toward the first plant, his eyes on the trees across the field.

The ground gave slightly beneath his right foot. He did not hear the spring click. What he heard was metal striking against bone. Pain flamed up Lanny's leg to consume his whole body.

When he came to, he was on the ground, his face inches from a pot plant. This ain't nothing but a bad dream, he told himself, thinking that if he believed it hard enough it might become true. He used his forearm to lift his head enough to look at the leg and the leg twisted slightly and the pain hit him like a fist. The world turned deep blue and he thought he was going to pass out again, but in a few moments the pain eased a little.

He looked at his foot and immediately wished he hadn't. The trap's jaws clenched around his leg just above the ankle. Blood soaked the tennis shoe red and he could see bone. Bile surged up from his stomach. Don't look at it any more until you have to, he told himself and lay his head back on the ground.

His face turned toward the sun now, and he guessed it was still early afternoon. Maybe it ain't that bad, he told himself. Maybe if I just lay here awhile it'll ease up some and I can get the trap off. He lay still as possible, breathing long, shallow breaths, trying to think about something else. He remembered what Old Man Jenkins had said about how one man could pretty much fish out a stream of speckled trout by himself if he took a notion to. Lanny wondered how many speckled trout he'd be able to catch out of Caney Creek before they were all gone. He wondered if after he did he'd be able to find another way-back trickle of water that held them.

He must have passed out again, because when he opened his eyes the sun hovered just above the tree line. When he tested the leg, it caught fire every bit as fierce as before. He wondered how late it would be tonight before his parents got worried and how long it would take after that before someone found his truck and people started searching. Tomorrow at the earliest, he told himself, and even then they'd search the river before looking anywhere else.

He lifted his head a few inches and shouted toward the woods. No one called back, and he imagined Linwood Toomey and his son passed-out drunk in their farmhouse. Being so close to the ground muffled his voice, so he used a forearm to raise himself a little higher and called again.

I'm going to have to sit up, he told himself, and just the thought of doing so made the bile rise again in his throat. He took deep breaths and used both arms to lift himself into a sitting position. The pain smashed against his body but just as quickly eased. The world began draining itself of color until everything around him seemed shaded with gray. He leaned back on the ground, sweat popping out on his face and arms like blisters. Everything seemed farther away, the sky and trees and plants, as though he were being lowered into a well. He shivered and wondered why he hadn't brought a sweatshirt with him.

Two men came out of the woods. They walked toward him with no more hurry than men come to check their tobacco for cutworms. Lanny knew the big man in front was Linwood Toomey and the man trailing him his son. He could not remember the son's name but had seen him in town a few times. What he remembered was that the son had been away from the county for nearly a decade and that some said he'd been in the marines and others said prison. The younger man wore a dirty white T-shirt and jeans, the older blue coveralls with no shirt underneath. Grease coated their hands and arms.

They stood above him but did not speak. Linwood Toomey took a rag from his back pocket and rubbed his hands and wrists. Lanny wondered if they weren't there at all, were nothing but some imagining the hurting caused.

"My leg's broke," Lanny said, figuring if they replied they must be real.

"It may well be," Linwood Toomey said. "I reckon it's near about cut clear off."

The younger man spoke.

"What we going to do?"

Linwood Toomey did not answer the question but eased himself onto the ground. They were almost eye level now.

"Who's your people?"

"My daddy's James Burgess. My momma was Ruthie Candler before she got married."

Linwood Toomey smiled.

"I know your daddy. Me and him used to drink some together, but that was back when he was sowing his wild oats. I'm still sowing mine, but I switched from oats. Found something that pays more."

Linwood Toomey stuffed the rag in his back pocket.

"You found it too."

"I reckon I need me a doctor," Lanny said. He was feeling better now, knowing Linwood Toomey was there beside him. His leg didn't hurt nearly as much now as it had before, and he told himself he could probably walk on it if he had to once Linwood Toomey got the trap off.

"What we going to do?" the son said again.

The older man looked up.

"We're going to do what needs to be done."

Linwood Toomey looked back at Lanny. He spoke slowly and his voice was soft.

"Coming back up here a second time took some guts, son. Even if I'd have figured out you was the one done it I'd have let it go, just for the feistiness of your doing such a thing. But coming a third time was downright foolish, and greedy. You're old enough to know better."

"I'm sorry," Lanny said.

Linwood Toomey reached out his hand and gently brushed some of the dirt off Lanny's face.

"I know you are, son."

Lanny liked the way Linwood Toomey spoke. The words were soothing, like rain on a tin roof. He was forgetting something, something important he needed to tell Linwood Toomey. Then he remembered.

"I reckon we best get on to the doctor, Mr. Toomey."

"There's no rush, son," Linwood Toomey said. "The doctor won't do nothing but finish cutting that lower leg off. We got to harvest these plants first. What if we was to take you down to the hospital and the law started wondering why we'd set a bear trap. They might figure there's something up here we wanted to keep folks from poking around and finding."

Linwood Toomey's words had started to blur and swirl in Lanny's mind. They were hard to hold in place long enough to make sense. But what he did understand was Linwood Toomey's words weren't said in a smart-ass way like Leonard Hamby's or Lanny's teachers' or spoken like he was still a child the way his parents' were. Lanny wanted to explain to Linwood Toomey how much he appreciated that, but to do so would mean having several sentences of words to pull apart from one another, and right now that was just too many. He tried to think of a small string of words he might untangle.

Linwood Toomey took a flat glass bottle from his back pocket and uncapped it.

"Here, son," he said, holding the bottle to Lanny's lips.

Lanny gagged slightly but kept most of the whiskey down.

He tried to remember what had brought him this far up the creek. Linwood Toomey pressed the bottle to his lips again.

"Take another big swallow," he said. "It'll cut the pain while you're waiting."

Lanny did as he was told and felt the whiskey spread down into his belly. It was warm and soothing, like an extra quilt on a cold night. Lanny thought of something he could say in just a few words.

"You reckon you could get that trap off my foot?"

"Sure," Linwood Toomey said. He slid over a few feet to reach the trap, then looked up at his son.

"Step on that lever, Hubert, and I'll get his leg out."

The pain rose up Lanny's leg again but it seemed less a part of him now. It seemed to him Linwood Toomey's words had soothed the bad hurting away.

"That's got it," Linwood Toomey said.

"Now what?" the son said.

"Go call Edgar and tell him we'll be bringing plants sooner than we thought. Bring back them machetes and we'll get this done."

The younger man walked toward the house.

"The whiskey help that leg some?" Linwood Toomey asked.

"Yes sir," Lanny mumbled, his eyes now closed. Even though Linwood Toomey was beside him, the man seemed to be drifting away along with the pain.

Linwood Toomey said something else but each word was like a balloon slipped free from Lanny's grasp. Then there was silence except for the gurgle of the creek, and Lanny remembered it was the speckled trout that had brought him here. He thought of how you could not see the orange fins and red flank spots but only the dark backs in the rippling water, and how it was only when they lay gasping on the green bank moss that you realized how bright and pretty they were.

❖